A Frenchman roams the vines at Ashton Estate Winery. He takes notes. He seduces the owner's niece….

No, it is not a plot to sabotage the Ashton Estate Winery. Nor is it the premise of a made-for-TV movie. It is Ashton Estate Winery's real-life attempt to improve their already popular wines—well, except for the part about seducing Spencer Ashton's niece!

Alexandre Dupree, a successful winemaker from France, has been consulting at Ashton Estate for several weeks. This, one can only assume, is to counteract the growing popularity of their rival winery, Louret Vineyards.

However, seducing Charlotte Ashton, Ashton Estate's florist, seems to be a strictly extracurricular activity. But we wonder, would Uncle Spencer approve? Or is he ruthless enough to use his own niece as the means to his own ends?

Dear Reader,

This May, Silhouette Desire's sensational lineup starts with Nalini Singh's *Awaken the Senses*. This DYNASTIES: THE ASHTONS title is a tale of sexual awakening starring one seductive Frenchman. (Can you say ooh-la-la?) Also for your enjoyment this month is the launch of Maureen Child's trilogy. The THREE-WAY WAGER series focuses on the Reilly brothers, triplets who bet each other they can stay celibate for ninety days. But wait until brother number one is reunited with *The Tempting Mrs. Reilly*.

Susan Crosby's BEHIND CLOSED DOORS series continues with *Heart of the Raven,* a gothic-toned story of a man whose self-imposed seclusion has cut him off from love…until a sultry woman, and a beautiful baby, open up his heart. Brenda Jackson is back this month with a new Westmoreland story, in *Jared's Counterfeit Fiancée,* the tale of a fake engagement that leads to real passion. Don't miss Cathleen Galitz's *Only Skin Deep,* a delightful transformation story in which a shy girl finally falls into bed with the man she's always dreamed about. And rounding out the month is *Bedroom Secrets* by Michelle Celmer, featuring a hero to die for.

Thanks for choosing Silhouette Desire, where we strive to bring you the best in smart, sensual romances. And in the months to come look for a new installment of our TEXAS CATTLEMAN'S CLUB continuity and a brand-new TANNERS OF TEXAS title from the incomparable Peggy Moreland.

Happy reading!

Melissa Jeglinski

Melissa Jeglinski
Senior Editor
Silhouette Books

Please address questions and book requests to:
Silhouette Reader Service
U.S.: 3010 Walden Ave., P.O. Box 1325, Buffalo, NY 14269
Canadian: P.O. Box 609, Fort Erie, Ont. L2A 5X3

AWAKEN THE SENSES

Nalini Singh

Published by Silhouette Books
America's Publisher of Contemporary Romance

Special thanks and acknowledgment are given to Nalini Singh
for her contribution to the DYNASTIES: THE ASHTONS series.

This one's for all my buddies in RWNZ.
I'd be lost without your support, humor and encouragement.

I'd also like to acknowledge the assistance provided by the following
people during my research for this book: Cheryl Heermann,
Gordon Lindsay, Melissa Moraven, Tom O'Sullivan and Sarah Stephenson.
Any mistakes are courtesy of this author and her artistic license.

 SILHOUETTE BOOKS

ISBN 0-373-76651-3

AWAKEN THE SENSES

Copyright © 2005 by Harlequin Books S.A.

Visit Silhouette Books at www.eHarlequin.com

Printed in U.S.A.

Books by Nalini Singh

Silhouette Desire

Desert Warrior #1529
Awaken to Pleasure #1602
Awaken the Senses #1651

NALINI SINGH

has always wanted to be a writer. Along the way to her dream, she obtained degrees in both the arts and law (because being a starving writer didn't appeal). After a short stint as a lawyer, she sold her first book and from that point, there was no going back. Now an escapee from the corporate world, she is looking forward to a lifetime of writing, interspersed with as much travel as possible. Currently residing in Japan, Nalini loves to hear from readers. You can contact her via the following e-mail address: nalini@nalinisingh.com; or by writing to her c/o Silhouette Books, 233 Broadway, Suite 1001, New York, NY 10279.

THE ASHTONS

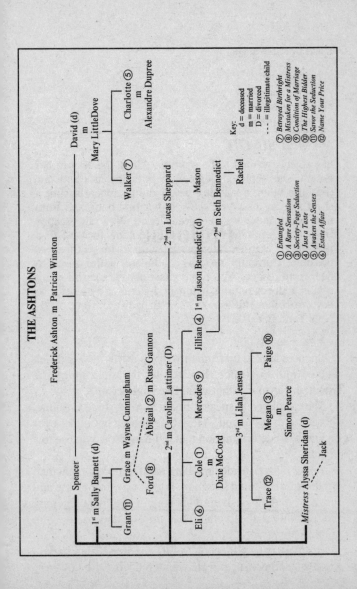

Frederick Ashton m Patricia Winston

David (d)
m
Mary LittleDove

Walker ⑦

Charlotte ⑤
m
Alexandre Dupree

Spencer

1ˢᵗ m Sally Barnett (d)

Grant ⑪

Grace m Wayne Cunningham

Abigail ② m Russ Gannon

Ford ⑧

2ⁿᵈ m Caroline Lattimer (D)

Cole ①
m
Dixie McCord

Mercedes ⑨

Jillian ④ 1ˢᵗ m Jason Bennedict (d)

2ⁿᵈ m Lucas Sheppard

Mason

2ⁿᵈ m Seth Bennedict

Rachel

Eli ⑥

3ʳᵈ m Lilah Jensen

Trace ⑫

Megan ③
m
Simon Pearce

Paige ⑩

Mistress Alyssa Sheridan (d)

Jack

Key:
d = deceased
m = married
D = divorced
- - - = illegitimate child

① Entangled
② A Rare Sensation
③ Society-Page Seduction
④ Just a Taste
⑤ Awaken the Senses
⑥ Estate Affair
⑦ Betrayed Birthright
⑧ Mistaken for a Mistress
⑨ Condition of Marriage
⑩ The Highest Bidder
⑪ Savor the Seduction
⑫ Name Your Price

Prologue

Thirty-One Years Ago

"We need to talk."

Spencer looked up from the papers on his desk as Lilah walked into his office. Irritated by the interruption, he frowned. Normally, that would've shut her up.

She continued to speak. "If you don't divorce Caroline, I'm going to leave you." Her voice shook, but in her eyes he glimpsed determination that felt dangerously close to a threat.

Anger blazed inside him, dark and far more violent than anything Lilah could summon. It took no effort to rise and move around the desk until his body was almost touching the reed-thin redhead who'd had the audacity to give him an ultimatum.

Her blue eyes widened. Tall as she was, Lilah had no trouble meeting his gaze. He wondered what she saw there that gave her the courage to straighten her spine. If she'd understood the depth of his fury, the silly chit would've been cowering in fear.

"You're beautiful, Lilah." He saw her pride awaken and almost laughed at how easy it was to manipulate her. "But the second you walk out that door—" he thrust in the verbal knife and twisted "—ten nubile young things will be standing there begging for my attention."

He enjoyed Lilah, enjoyed her body and her face, enjoyed the way she gave in to all of his wishes. Completely under his spell, she would do anything he asked. Now, he watched her swallow and savored the sight of her already shaky confidence seeping out of her.

"I mean it, I want you to leave Caroline." Though that husky, little-girl voice shook, her blue eyes sparked with possessiveness. "You've been with her for six years—it's my turn now."

The sexual attraction he felt for her flared at this display of just how much she wanted him, but coldly, clinically, he squelched it. "And if I don't?" His voice had gone quiet. A warning.

Her slender shoulders squared. "Then I'm going to find another man. You can hire yourself a new…secretary." The last word was a taunt.

Nobody walked away from Spencer Ashton. *Nobody.* Certainly not a female whom he'd bedded and had yet to tire of. Reaching out with one hand, he grasped her hair and pulled her body hard against his, not caring if he hurt her. When he tugged her head back, her eyes met his, fear dawning in the blue.

Tightening his grasp, he leaned in very close and whispered, "What did you say?"

She whimpered as he pulled her head even further back. "I'm s-sorry, Spencer. I d-didn't mean it."

The panic in her eyes acted as an aphrodisiac. He was suddenly very sure that he was going to have Lilah Jensen spread out under him within a few minutes. "Good." He ran his finger down her throat. "What was that about leaving me if I didn't leave Caroline?" Her skin was soft under his spreading hand, her neck fragile.

"I—I'm s-sorry," she said again. "I'll make it up to you." Tentatively, her hands touched his chest, beginning to undo buttons. "It's just that I want you s-so much."

He smiled, aware that she really did want him that much. She *was* a beautiful thing, he acknowledged. And very accommodating in bed. He might end up marrying her after he got rid of Caroline, but that was for him to decide. Lilah had to learn her place here and now, before he gave her anything, much less the right to bear his name.

"I'll do anything you want, Spencer." Lilah's blue gaze was a little less afraid, a little more sexually enticing.

He found the combination seductive, but despite her charms, he wanted her to be very, very aware that this had been her last chance. Keeping one hand clenched in her hair, while the other moved to rest over her breast, he whispered, "A lot of people have tried to threaten me over the years." He kept his voice casual, thrillingly aware of the power he held over this woman.

Her lips parted as she tried to speak. He squeezed her throat slightly. She shut up.

"Not a single one has succeeded in turning threat into reality. *Not a single one.*" He smiled gently and leaned down to kiss her parted lips. "Do we understand each other?"

Lilah nodded, not attempting to speak. He liked her total consent to his will, liked that she'd finally acknowledged and accepted the place she occupied in his life. To him, she was property. He owned her like he owned his car and his home.

Lust awakened inside him, fed by the fuel of her fear and perhaps even by the way she wanted him. Pressing her closer, he said, "Now...why don't you show me how sorry you are."

One

Alexandre wondered if he'd made a mistake in accepting Trace Ashton's invitation to stay at the estate. It had seemed like the convenient option, given that he'd be spending large amounts of time at the Ashton Estate Winery in the coming weeks.

His arrival last night had been unremarkable. The elegant Lilah Jensen Ashton had welcomed him to her showcase of a home and ensured that he was comfortable. Spencer Ashton hadn't made an appearance, but having met the man previously, Alexandre hadn't been the least disappointed. The Ashton patriarch was an arrogant bastard who Alexandre didn't particularly care for. Of course, he thought with cynical amusement, some would apply the same label to him.

He stalked through rows of vines bathed in the early morning sunshine, still dewed with the light rain that had fallen earlier. The soil was a rich brown, the entire vineyard full of life. Fresh green leaves covered the ropey vines and flowering was well in progress. He paused for a second to examine some of the flowers, judging that fruit set would begin soon. But the thought didn't distract him for long, his mind still on his living arrangements.

Though he was an early riser, this morning his slumber had been interrupted by loud voices in the second floor hallway. Soon after he'd come fully awake, a door had slammed and shut out the altercation, but what he'd heard had been enough to tell him that Lilah and Spencer's marriage wasn't exactly on solid ground.

The fact that just before he'd left for this walk he'd seen Spencer drive off at a furious speed, had only cemented his conclusion. That realization didn't particularly throw him off his stride. He'd seen far worse society marriages. But, if this morning had been any indication, it was highly likely that the atmosphere in the house was going to be uncomfortable during his stay.

His other concern was that he might inadvertently become privy to family matters when he had no desire to get caught up in the turmoil surrounding the Ashtons. He was here to advise Trace on the estate's winemaking processes—nothing more. Frowning, he knelt down between the vines, testing the soil with his fingertips. The gesture was instinctive, barely impinging on his thoughts.

As a stranger, he didn't understand all the emotional undercurrents running through the house, but he could make an educated guess given the scandal that had erupted last month relating to Spencer's first marriage.

Alexandre was a winemaker, not a socialite, but it had proved impossible to avoid hearing that bit of news. His *maman* thought it her business to keep him informed of his business rivals' and friends' weaknesses. He smiled at the thought of the woman who'd been the only constant in his life, such as she was, flaws and all.

A strange sound, followed by sudden movement to his left, caught his attention, shifting his thoughts away from his troubled hosts. Irritated at the prospect of having his solitude disturbed, he paused in the act of rising to his feet, wondering who else was awake at this hour. Seeking privacy, he'd deliberately walked away from the main house and the likelihood of company.

"Why are you making that funny noise?" a soft female voice asked. "I gave you a full checkup yesterday!"

Eyebrows raised, Alexandre stood and stepped out of the vines into a narrow abutting lane that he hadn't noticed earlier. The cause of the disturbance was immediately visible. Delight replaced his earlier irritation. Now, this wake-up call was far more to his liking.

She was petite, he thought—her body small but with no lack of curves. One of those lush curves was currently outlined beautifully by well-worn denim as she knelt on the ground and peered at the front wheel of her bicycle. Long, arrow-straight black hair shifted like thick silk as she moved, brushing her bottom again and again.

Interest sparked low and deep in his gut, a sharp hunger that was at odds with the jaded boredom that had crept up on him over the past year. "Do you need assistance, *mon amie?*"

Charlotte spun around so fast, she almost toppled her bike. Not having expected anyone else to be up and about, she was startled to find herself looking up into the most gorgeous male face she'd ever seen.

An amused light in his dark eyes, the stranger held out a long-fingered hand. "My apologies. I didn't mean to startle you."

Swallowing, she let him help her to her feet. His hand was strong, his fingers curling around her own until she felt engulfed…owned. Heat sizzled up her spine and burned through her cheeks. She tugged her hand away the moment she was up, unable to cope with the explosive fire shooting through her body.

"We haven't been introduced," he said, his voice accented in a way that was so very deliciously French, her knees threatened to give out. "I'm Alexandre Dupree."

Alexandre. It suited him. A strong, masculine name for a man who was just that.

"Char—Charlotte," she managed to say around the lump of fascination stuck in her throat.

"Charlotte," he repeated, and on his lips, her ordinary name was suddenly exotic. "And what are you doing here so very early, *petite* Charlotte? You work on the estate, *oui?*"

Perhaps she should've been insulted that he thought her a worker, rather than a member of the privileged Ashton family, but then she'd never wanted to be a member of that family. "No." She hadn't ever met a man like him, one who exuded sexuality like other men breathed. It made rational thought difficult.

"No?" His full lips curved into a coaxing smile that was just this side of sinful. "You wish to be a mystery?"

"What about you?" she blurted out, the compulsion to know more about him overcoming her nervous shyness.

Who was this man who'd smiled at her and in a single moment succeeded in shaking all her beliefs about her own ability to experience passion and desire? She could feel her body sparking with life, embers of something hot and sensual glowing deep inside her. It was as if she'd been waiting for this man since the day she'd become a woman. Was it any wonder no one else had ever measured up?

His eyes, dark as the bitterest chocolate, lingered on her lips and she wanted to ask him to stop, but the words wouldn't come. It felt like he was kissing her with noth-

ing more than a look, making her feel things that should
be illegal this early in the morning.

"I am working with Trace Ashton."

A winemaker, she thought, well aware of Trace's am-
bition to produce award-winning Ashton Estate vintages.
Yet, Alexandre didn't appear to be anyone's idea of an employee. Though he was dressed casually in black slacks and
an open-necked white shirt with the sleeves rolled up, she
could tell that the clothing was of the finest quality, as was
the steel watch strapped to his wrist.

"Where do you go, *ma chérie?*" He looked down the
pathway, where it curved through the vines. "Would you
like some company on your journey?"

Her eyes widened. "N-no," she stuttered, flustered by
the charm of his smile, the sinful beauty of his eyes. "I—
I have to go. I'm late." Straddling her bike, she pushed off
the kickstand and began to pedal away.

Crackle, clunk, crackle.

Her face flushed as the noise sounded, a reminder of
why she'd stopped in the first place. Halting, she was about
to get off when she became aware that Alexandre had
moved in close.

"Stay, Charlotte. I can see the problem." Leaning down,
he twisted the back reflector, his strong fingers making
quick work of the task. "It had shifted so it rubbed against
the spokes of the wheel," he explained when he saw her
peering over her shoulder.

Another blush heated her cheeks. She knew that even
her darker skin tone wouldn't have hidden that appallingly
vivid indication of her complete inability to deal with him.
"Thank you."

"You are welcome. *Bon voyage.*" The teasing smile accompanying his words made her want to bite her lip. Or
maybe she wanted to bite his…

Taking a ragged breath, she started pedaling, aware of his gaze on her back until she turned the corner. Only then did she exhale and allow herself to think back over the knee-trembling encounter.

Had he been flirting with her?

A second later, she shook her head at that silly idea. Men as deliciously sexy as Alexandre Dupree didn't flirt with shy gardeners like her. But for the first time in forever, Charlotte found herself wishing that a charming, sophisticated and way-out-of-her-league male had indeed been flirting with her.

Alexandre couldn't stop thinking about his early-morning encounter as he went through the day. A bit of subtle investigation on his part had revealed two surprising bits of information. His shy beauty was an Ashton—Charlotte Ashton to be precise.

Her connection to the troubled Ashtons should've made him wary, but he was intrigued instead. The woman he'd met had been easily flustered and uneasy in his presence, yet she was a member of this privileged family.

Not only that, she operated the successful greenhouse located on the Ashton Estate. It was Trace who inadvertently gave him that information while showing him a map of the estate.

"This is Charlotte's greenhouse." Trace tapped at the outline of a building located about two miles east of the estate house. "That's the cottage and her design studio's here."

"A greenhouse?" Alexandre tried to keep his tone casual. "What is it for?"

"Charlotte does all the floral arrangements for events held on the estate. That greenhouse is her baby." The usually reserved Trace smiled. "You should go have a look— I'm sure she wouldn't mind giving you a tour."

"How do I get to Charlotte's greenhouse?" he asked, savoring the taste of her name on his lips.

"Take one of the golf carts—the path's easy to navigate."

Charlotte obviously preferred to ride her misbehaving bicycle. Alexandre smiled inwardly at the idea of tracking her to her territory. Perhaps surrounded by her flowers, she'd be more relaxed with him…more willing to entertain the ideas uncurling in the most male part of his psyche.

Work commitments meant that he didn't get a chance to seek out Charlotte until well after lunch. Around three o'clock, he commandeered a golf cart and headed east. Once he got closer, the greenhouse was easy to find, rising clearly above the vines.

He parked in front of the first building, a stone cottage surrounded by gardens full of wildflowers. Reminiscent of something out of a fairy tale, it perfectly fit the woman whom he'd surprised this morning. Small, a little fey and ultimately enchanting.

Just behind the cottage sat the greenhouse, with another building set close up against its right side. The sign on the smaller building proclaimed it to be Ashton Estate Botanicals, clearly the design studio Trace had pointed out.

Expecting Charlotte to be working in the greenhouse, he walked that way. His whole body sighed as he entered and saw her. Dressed in faded jeans that faithfully caressed every feminine curve and a short-sleeved pink shirt, she looked as fresh as the flowers blooming around her. The silky waterfall of her hair was plaited in one long rope, the end brushing across her bottom as she moved back and forth.

Her back was to him as she worked at the heavy wooden workbench set up in the middle of the greenhouse. It looked like she was repotting. She liked working surrounded by the flowers she nurtured, he thought to himself.

Suddenly, though he hadn't made a sound, she whirled around, a small trowel held aggressively in her gloved hand. Her big eyes appeared to get even bigger as she saw him. "What are you doing here?"

"I came to find my mysterious little *fleur*." He eyed the trowel she still held pointed to his heart.

Blushing, she put it on the bench behind her. "Why?"

"Are you always so direct?" He prowled closer, liking the look of her even more than he had earlier today. She was certainly small, but she was most perfectly a woman. In the past, he'd tended to go for long-limbed beauties. Looking at Charlotte, he couldn't understand why. "It's very warm in here. You do not mind?"

"It's to help the flowers grow out of season." She watched him as he approached, as wary as a wild deer. "I like the heat."

His eye fell on a small blue notebook on her bench. "What do you write in there?" he asked curiously.

He could've sworn panic turned her eyes black. "It's my g-gardening journal."

Obviously, he'd misread her reaction. "It smells like sunshine and growth in here," he murmured, slowing his pace but not changing direction.

"What do you want?" she repeated, pressing back against the bench as if she wanted to blend into it.

"You don't like me, *ma petite?*" He wondered if for once, his sense about women had let him down. He'd never been one to push where he wasn't wanted, and certainly not with women. They were to be indulged, cosseted and coaxed, not forced. To his shock, he realized that if this woman didn't want him, he'd have a very hard time walking away.

Her gold-dust skin suffused with pink. "I didn't say that."

Scenting victory, he prowled closer, lifting a finger to touch one warm cheek. *"Non?"*

"I…" She stepped sideways, breaking contact. "Please, this is my space."

"And you wish me to leave." Though not a man who gave up easily, he had no wish to cause her any hurt.

Perhaps, he acknowledged, she'd seen the truth he'd been avoiding since the first moment she'd stared at him with those big brown eyes—at thirty-four he was far too old and jaded for her. This woman was as fresh and beautiful as the blooms she tended, and he'd lost his innocence a long, long time ago.

Fighting the urge to touch her again, he sketched a half-bow. "Then I'll go. I apologize for disturbing you." He turned and took the first steps to the door, feeling an unaccountable sense of loss.

"Wait!"

Pausing, he looked over his shoulder. Charlotte closed the gap between them and without meeting his gaze, held out a fragile white blossom. "Put this in your room. It'll make it smell like sunshine and…growth."

Startled at the gift and her recall of his words, he took the flower. "*Merci*, Charlotte. I don't believe anyone has ever given me flowers before." Lifting the bloom to his nose, he breathed in the fragrance.

Her lips curved in a tentative smile. "You're welcome."

And suddenly, he knew he was. All his confidence returned twofold. So, little Charlotte Ashton wasn't averse to him. She just wasn't comfortable in his presence. Alexandre couldn't understand why. She was a lovely, beautiful flower, as exotic as the orchids she grew in this glass garden. Beautiful women had always liked Alexandre, for they knew he was a man who appreciated them.

In truth, *most* women liked him because he genuinely liked them, respecting the steel spines beneath many of their fragile fronts. Charlotte, he thought, probably had a spine steelier than any of them. It took determination and hard work to nurture life and her greenhouse was bursting at the seams with it. Even more, it must've taken strength to follow a different path in this family dedicated to wine and business. His *maman* would like her.

"Tell me about your greenhouse," he coaxed.

Her cheeks bloomed with color but on that topic at least, she was willing to talk. "I grow lots of things in here, from daisies to ferns."

"I can see gardens behind your bench," he said, truly intrigued. "How can you grow things in the ground inside a greenhouse?"

Her eyes brightened. "The earth in that part is exposed. Small pebbles on the floor facilitate drainage."

"Show me," he said softly, seduced by the confidence in her eyes.

After the tiniest hesitation, she turned and walked back through the rows of high tables set with trays overflowing with blooms. He followed, keeping enough distance that she didn't feel crowded. As they walked, he had to duck a few times to avoid the greenery growing downward from the considerable number of hanging baskets.

After they circled her workbench, Charlotte pointed to the lush green garden on the left. "These are my ferns." The ferns were overflowing onto a small wooden bench placed next to the garden.

"And over here—" she moved to the opposite side "—are my tropical blooms. Smell this." Shyness lingered in her eyes but her lips were curved.

Undone, he leaned forward and inhaled the heady fragrance from a creamy white flower, its heart shaded with strokes of sunny yellow. "It makes me want to be on a South Sea beach."

Her smile of delight tumbled his heart. "It's *Plumeria*—frangipani. One whiff and I'm lost in dreams."

Something fell into place. "That's the scent you wear." It had been haunting him since this morning.

Big eyes widened in surprise. "Yes. I order it from the Pacific."

A sense of intimacy invaded the air. Before it could get heavy and alarm her, he asked, "What else grows here?"

She looked relieved. "Next to the frangipani is a hibiscus I've been babying for a year. It's being stubborn about blooming."

He chuckled. "Perhaps it is like you, wishing to be mysterious."

Her lashes drifted down. "I'm just me. Nothing mysterious at all."

"I disagree." Encouraged by the light in her eyes, he took a chance. "Today, I must return to my work, but will you have dinner with me tomorrow?"

All her sweet confidence disappeared under a veil of reserve. "I...I've got plans. Th—thank you for asking." She busied herself with pulling off her gloves.

He wanted to reach over and kiss her, melt her resistance with a gentle seduction. "Ah, *ma chérie,* you break my heart. Perhaps you will reconsider, *non?* If you change your mind, I'm staying at the estate house." With those lighthearted words, he headed out of the greenhouse, her gift held gently in his hand.

Now that he knew she didn't abhor his presence, he had no intention of giving up on his shy blossom. He just wished he knew what to do to win her trust. Given the jaded nature of his own heart, he'd made it a point to stay away from innocents. But, for some reason, he couldn't stay away from this one with her big brown eyes and blushing cheeks.

He knew she was too soft and young for him, but he also knew that he wasn't going to walk away. Instead, he was going to break every single one of his rules and seduce her, seduce her so completely that those brown eyes wouldn't even look at another man ever again.

A frown creased his brow at the commitment implied in that sudden thought. He had no intention of marrying, not when he knew the frailties of the institution so very well, and Charlotte was the marrying kind. A woman made for a lifetime of loving.

His scowl intensified. Why were his thoughts heading in such directions? Seduction and sensory pleasure were all he ever promised a woman. Charlotte's wariness around him told him that she understood that instinctively. He'd never lie to her about his intentions, but he *would* have her.

What most women failed to detect beneath his charming front was a determination that made a thunderstorm look weak by comparison. Once set on a course, Alexandre Dupree would not deviate from it unless it suited his purpose. And right now, he was set on sweet little Charlotte Ashton.

Two

Safe inside her greenhouse, Charlotte watched Alexandre get into the stylish golf cart and drive away.

"Oh, my," she whispered, when he was finally out of sight. The man was lethal. Those dark eyes, that charming smile and especially that way he had of looking at her like he'd like to devour her—they all added up to a combination that spelled danger. Charlotte wasn't the kind of woman with whom dangerous men played.

Rubbing her hands on her jeans, she swallowed at the thought of actually accepting Alexandre's dinner invitation. A second later, she discarded the idea. Except for when discussing her beloved plants, the one topic about which she had complete confidence, she could barely speak in his presence. The pressure of a date would undoubtedly leave her tongue-tied.

Pain shot through her at the reminder of her shortcomings. She was probably the only Ashton on the estate who couldn't hold her own in the kind of sophisticated environment they inhabited. That was why she'd retreated to her flowers. They didn't expect anything from her but kindness.

She knew she was partly at fault for her social inability. If she'd stayed in the big house, she could've learned the necessary skills from Lilah.

Her lips thinned.

Sure, Lilah would've loved teaching the niceties of mingling in society to the half-breed brat who'd been foisted on her. The elegant redhead had always quietly hated the fact that she'd been saddled with the responsibility of raising two children of mixed parentage. Being so enamored of Spencer, Charlotte's brother Walker hadn't much noticed her subtle antipathy. But Charlotte had needed a woman in her life and Lilah had made sure Charlotte knew she could never expect that woman to be Spencer's wife.

Shaking her head, she returned to the seedlings she'd been repotting. Perhaps she could ask Jillian for advice, she thought, sinking one gloved hand into a bag of soil. There was a grace about her older cousin that would've normally intimidated Charlotte, but Jillian also had such warmth that she'd found herself wanting to tell the slender brunette things she rarely told anyone.

Like her belief that her mother was still alive.

For the past few months, that belief had grown stronger and stronger, until she was almost bursting with the need to share it. Since the secret of Spencer's first marriage had come out, her belief had turned into a certainty. If the man could lie once, why not twice?

Though she wanted to share her thoughts, she'd barely been able to broach the topic even with Jillian. Confiding the details would require a level of trust that Charlotte couldn't bring herself to give to anyone.

She shook her head at her own wandering thoughts.

"You have to finish the repotting." Despite the order, her mind kept returning to the topic and she knew why. It was because she'd stalled in her search. Not because she didn't know how to go forward but because she was afraid.

What she found could change her life forever. Going alone and unsupported into the unknown frightened her. After years of hard work, she'd managed to create a haven on this estate where she'd never felt at home. The thought of losing this feeling of safety to the cruel truth terrified her.

Alexandre Dupree had surely never been afraid, never been a coward like her, she thought, unable to keep her mind from drifting to the charming Frenchman who'd walked into her life and far too quickly begun to fascinate her.

He reminded her of all the things she could never be. The man exuded charisma with every breath, as dangerously beautiful as a stalking leopard. His sensuality alone was powerful enough, but once you added the razor sharp mind hidden behind the charm, he became the most fascinating creature she'd ever met.

She guessed his lazy charm fooled many people into thinking him a playboy. She knew better. After meeting him that morning, she'd logged onto the Internet and done some research. Alexandre Dupree was no playboy. He was one of the most respected winemakers in the world. The only reason she hadn't heard his name before now was that her plants interested her far more than the vineyards and their produce. That was Trace's passion.

Not only was he a respected winemaker, Alexandre was a rich one. Filthy rich. The most public of his successful commercial interests was the small winery he owned in France, but she'd also found his name mentioned in relation to several exclusive restaurants. It made sense that a man famed for producing "wines of stunning complexity" should choose to align himself with places that served food fit for his wines.

What made him extraordinary was that instead of hoarding it, he didn't begrudge others his expertise. Witness his presence here, helping Trace find just the right texture, the right taste, to tempt the most fussy of palates.

If Alexandre's wealth and skill hadn't been enough to intimidate her, she'd found several photos of him at high profile events. He'd been photographed at the Cannes Film Festival several times, always accompanied by a leggy, sharply elegant creature in a killer dress. Not only did his women have several inches in height on Charlotte, they had "breeding" stamped on their perfect profiles, elegance oozing out of their perfect pores and grace flowing from their every perfect movement.

Shaking her head at her inability to banish the Frenchman to a corner of her mind, she finished off the final pot and quickly tidied up. When she walked into her cottage to take a shower, the first thing she saw was the picture of Alexandre she'd printed out that morning. Frustrated with her susceptibility to the man, she strode into the shower, hoping the water would wash away her inexplicable fascination.

Fifteen minutes later, she stepped out of the humid glass cube and shrugged into a fluffy white robe. As she stood in front of her bedroom mirror, combing her towel-dried hair, her eyes didn't see the woman she'd become but the painfully shy girl she'd been.

Unable to adapt fully to life with the Ashtons, she'd withdrawn into herself when Walker had begun to spend more and more time with Spencer. To the girl she'd been, it had felt like her uncle had stolen her brother from her…just like he'd stolen her mother.

The phone rang, startling her into dropping the brush. "Charlotte," she said, her voice a little husky.

"*Ma chérie,* what is wrong?"

Every nerve ending in her body went on high alert at that deep male voice. "Nothing."

A pause. "Have you changed your mind about dinner with me tomorrow?" His words were practical but his tone turned them into a caress…a question from one lover to another.

She knew she should reprimand him for the way he continued to speak to her so familiarly, but she couldn't find the words. "I…" The temptation to say yes was almost overwhelming, but fear held her back—she didn't know how to deal with a man like him. Only in her dreams could she be witty and sophisticated enough for him. "No."

He sighed, as if she'd broken his heart. "Then perhaps I could persuade you into a walk?"

The hunger in her bucked at the reins. "A walk?"

As if sensing victory, his sinful voice became even more hauntingly seductive. "I'll come to your cottage tomorrow around six and we can take a walk through the vineyard. Say yes, Charlotte."

Sweat dampened her palms. "I'll be ready." She couldn't believe her own temerity.

"Until tomorrow then. Good night—sleep well."

As she hung up the phone, Charlotte wondered about the number of women who'd heard the same from him in far more intimate settings. Surely, a man as sensual as Alexandre had no lack of bed partners. Wrenching the brush through her hair, she told herself to stop obsessing.

Unfortunately, she couldn't control her dreams.

Alexandre spent the night alone, as he'd chosen to do for a considerable period of time. Though he had a healthy sexual appetite, simple physical pleasure had ceased to satisfy his needs.

He wanted something more, though if pressed, he wouldn't have been able to say exactly what it was that was missing from his life. He just knew that despite his sexual frustration, no woman had tempted him to break his self-imposed celibacy.

Until now.

Charlotte Ashton had reawakened the craving, a craving sharper than ever before. He might've put the strength of his need down to his long period of abstinence, except that compared to the sensual shimmer between him and Charlotte, all his previous relationships had been mere shadows.

She was…unique, he thought, clasping his hands behind his head as he lay in the guest bedroom allocated to him by his hostess. Apparently, it had once been Walker Ashton's room. All traces of the other man were now gone. A pity, Alexandre mused. Perhaps he might've divined something about Charlotte from her brother.

Both his fascination and frustration with her had been mounting since this morning. For the first time in over a year, he'd seen a woman whom he couldn't get out of his head and she was as wary as a butterfly, as wide-eyed and innocent as a teenager. He wondered if she were truly as innocent as she appeared. Something low in him tightened in expectation and…possession.

Surprise had him sucking in a sharp breath.

Alexandre had never been a possessive man, had never wanted to be, not after the lessons of his childhood. He knew just how changeable women were, knew that a man couldn't rely on them, beautiful and lovely though they might be. While he'd appreciated and enjoyed their seductive femininity, he'd always kept a safe emotional distance between himself and his lovers.

Even the single time he'd forgotten that vow in the headlong rush of youthful emotion, part of him had remained separate. His fiancée, Celeste's defection had hurt him but he'd been far from devastated.

But now, a deeply slumbering part of him was waking and it felt like truth. This possessive tyrant was a part of his psyche that he'd forcibly restrained for a lifetime but it refused to be silenced any longer. The tyrant had sensed Charlotte's compelling scent and decided she belonged to him. Without compromise.

Smiling into the darkness, Alexandre accepted the possessiveness rushing through him, reveling in the powerful emotion after months of jaded weariness. This unabating hunger was uncharted territory, but he welcomed the dangers which lay ahead.

"Charlotte, *ma petite*," he whispered into the heavy darkness. "I shall enjoy our dance."

He spent most of the following day in discussions with James, the head winemaker. To Alexandre's relief, the other man was in no way threatened by his presence. James knew he was good at what he was employed to do—create popular Ashton wines. Alexandre's purpose at the estate was entirely different.

They began with an intensive tour of the winery, including the basement cellars. Alexandre was particularly interested in the nature and size of the barrels used to age Ashton vintages, given their affect on the amount of oxygen that reached the maturing wine.

The rest of the time was taken up with an investigation of the fermentation tanks and discussions on technical matters such as sulphurification and cooling. This was necessary background—before he could advise Trace about the future, he had to understand how the winery operated now.

When he finally called it a day, he had barely enough time for a quick shower before heading to Charlotte's. To his pleasure, she was waiting outside for him, checking things in the outdoor gardens that surrounded her enchanted cottage.

He walked over, taking in the exquisite sight of her in well-worn blue jeans and a short-sleeved white shirt. Detailed with lace and skimming close to her body, the shirt was enticingly feminine. *"Bonjour,* Charlotte.*"*

Having seen him arrive, she wasn't startled, but wariness shadowed her eyes. "Hi."

"Shall we?" With another woman, he would've touched her lower back, or perhaps taken her arm, but with Charlotte, he had a feeling that even such a small advance would be moving too fast.

After a minute hesitation, she began to walk beside him along the lane she used to cycle up to the estate house. There was more than enough daylight left for him to watch his intriguing, mysterious companion.

"You must know much about the vines, having grown up on the estate." He forced himself to keep his tone conversational and light despite the sensual tension that shivered between them.

Beside him, Charlotte moved her shoulders in a shrug that tried to be careless but was just a little too tense. At the same time, something flickered in her expression and he got the impression that she didn't like talking about the world she inhabited.

"I don't know that much." She looked up to meet his gaze. "It doesn't really interest me. I've picked up bits and pieces over the years."

"You're interested only in flowers?" He paused and she did the same, turning to face him.

"Not only. But mostly." A smile spread across her face. "I will admit that I love the vineyard at this time of year."

"Why?" He spoke softly, unwilling to trigger her previous wariness when she appeared to be relaxing.

"It's the fact that they're coming to life." Her fingers caressed the edges of a new leaf. Desire spiked—would she stroke her man as sweetly? "Everything's just beginning and there are so many possibilities in the air."

He was captivated by the fleeting glimpse of the woman hidden behind the self-contained quietness. "Yes, the possibilities are endless."

Her cheeks bloomed a soft pink and he knew she understood that they were no longer talking about the vines. Instead of shying away, she said, "The choices we make now have to be the right ones, though—otherwise the damage to the harvest could be substantial."

"Perhaps that's true," he said, delighted by her willingness to at least consider the idea of taking their relationship further. "But there are also times when chances must be taken."

"It's safer to follow the known path."

His lips quirked at the challenge. "Safe approaches produce palatability, nothing more. I prefer my wine to be far more full-bodied, a symphony of aroma and taste to delight the senses. Do you not, *chérie?*"

"Yes, I do." There was a dreamy sensuality to her voice that he knew had come about because of his words, and he reveled in it. "I don't know much about winemaking."

"I can teach you everything. Ask me any question you wish."

She parted her lips, as if to speak. And that was all it took. Awareness flashed to life between them, sudden and blinding. Her eyes widened but she didn't back away as he'd half expected. Instead, invitation trembled in the lushness of her mouth.

He'd told himself to be patient—to coax, not push—but at that moment he couldn't remember any of his own warnings. Desire washed over him in a powerful wave, obliterating caution. Reaching out, he cupped her cheek with one hand and bent his head. Without any prompting, her lips parted even further, disintegrating his control.

She was soft and tasted like his darkest dreams. The decadent flavor of her was at odds with her innocent eyes and it intoxicated him. He'd intended only a sip but found himself delving deeper, asking for more. For a stunning moment of sensory pleasure, she responded with desire as open and wild as his.

But the moment was far too short. Making a tiny sound, she jerked away. "What…?" Confusion muddled her gaze as she touched her kiss-wet lips with one trembling hand, the other flat on his chest.

He could see that she wasn't ready to deal with the implications arising from the stunning sensuality of their first kiss. The rapid entanglement of their senses had shaken him and he was by far the more experienced party. He couldn't blame her for looking like the world had just crumbled from under their feet.

"It was only a kiss." He kept his hands to his sides, though he wanted nothing more than to hold her. "It was of no moment." He'd meant to reassure her, but knew he'd said the wrong thing when she stumbled back a step, bruised hurt in her eyes.

"I'm afraid you have the wrong idea about me, Mr. Dupree." Tears glittered but her soft tone was suddenly without compromise. "Find another woman for your kisses of no moment. I'm not interested in relieving your boredom while you're here."

"*Charlotte.*" He wondered if she'd react any better to the truth—that though they'd barely met, he hungered for her like he'd never hungered for another woman.

From the instant he'd seen her, his body had recognized hers and ached for completion. What they'd felt in that kiss had been a sign of the sensual surrender to come, something his innocent lover was in no way prepared to accept.

"Don't." She began to back away toward her home. "I shouldn't have come with you."

The words cut him. "I would never harm you."

"It's what men like you do," she whispered and then she was gone.

He could've caught up in seconds but knew that any chase would be futile. She was in no mood to listen. In an attempt to protect her, he'd wounded her pride and made her feel less of a woman. And he was still smarting from her final words.

What did she know about men like him? Did she place him in the same category as Spencer Ashton? Anger flared. Shoving his hands in the pockets of his tan slacks, he began to stride back toward the estate house. He'd ask someone to come down tomorrow and retrieve the golf cart. Right now, he needed to work off both his anger and a fair dose of sexual tension.

It's what men like you do.

Maybe she was right. He had no intention of offering her forever, and she was the kind of woman for whom forever had been created.

But, as he'd decided last night, he wasn't going to let her push him away, either. Not when this thing between them blazed with life on both sides. Charlotte Ashton belonged to Alexandre Dupree—no matter what she'd tried to convince herself of after being singed by the heat of that kiss.

Three

Charlotte wasn't known for her temper, but she was good and mad as she entered the cottage and slammed the door. How dare he kiss her in a way that melted her bones and then say it was of no moment? How could he not have felt what she had? His reaction had humiliated her, made her feel like that gawky, lonely teenager all over again. And it had made her angry.

She might not be as sophisticated as him, but she had her pride and it wasn't something that she'd let any man disparage. As far as she was concerned, Alexandre Dupree could find himself a new toy. It no longer mattered that before their kiss, she'd found herself becoming more and more comfortable in his presence.

Oh, he'd still made her stomach flutter with nerves and her femininity sit up and take notice, but she'd begun to lose her shyness. Each time he'd turned those dark French eyes on her, she felt herself coming to life as a woman.

It was just as well that this had ended before it began. She'd said her final words to him in anger, but they were true. He was a powerful, experienced male used to beautiful women and discreet affairs. He'd break her heart if she let him near her.

After giving them both a night to calm down, Alexandre had intended to seek out Charlotte first thing that morning. However, the minute he appeared at breakfast, Trace informed him that an in-depth tour of the vineyard had been organized for him, to be followed later that afternoon by a tasting of Ashton wines.

Unwilling to reveal his interest in Charlotte and further complicate an already complicated situation, he accepted the plans with good grace. The tour of the vineyard calmed his soul. However, the tasting was a disaster—the sweet aroma of Charlotte filled his senses, allowing nothing else to filter through.

No woman had ever affected him like this. He wasn't sure he liked being fascinated so completely, but he *was* sure that he wanted the object of his fascination in his arms.

Finally free of all his obligations, he drove to the cottage as evening was falling. To his surprise, Charlotte wasn't home tucked up safe and warm. Frowning, he walked over to the greenhouse, wondering if she was babying her hothouse flowers.

However, only a single light burned in the greenhouse—it was unlikely she was there. He quickly walked around to make sure. Because of the layout, it was impossible to see from one end of the greenhouse to the other, especially toward the back where her gardens took over.

He was turning to leave the garden area when something shiny caught his eye. Curious, he retraced his steps. It took him a few moments to spot the blue note-

book half hidden beneath a trailing sweep of lush greenery. It lay on the small wooden bench beside the fern garden—the steel spine had reflected the light and captured
his attention.

Thinking that Charlotte wouldn't like it if her notes
got wet when the garden's sprinkler system activated, he
picked up the slender volume and slipped it into the inner
pocket of his lightweight jacket. He'd dressed semi-formal-
ly, intending to take Charlotte to dinner. He had every confidence in his ability to charm her out of her temper.

When he strode out, he was startled to see a light being
turned on in the cottage. Scowling, he crossed the distance
between the two buildings and knocked.

It swung open after a small pause. "What are you doing here?" she asked, eyes dark and unwelcoming.

He was hit by the utterly unsophisticated urge to haul
her to his chest and teach her to never again ask him such
a silly question. If she believed him to be a man who gave
up easily, then she was in for a surprise.

But used to keeping his emotions under control, he only leaned lazily against the doorjamb, crowding her back
into the house. "I came to see you, *ma petite*. You left me
in such anger yesterday—I didn't wish to cause you pain."

"You didn't. I'm fine."

Reaching up, he captured her chin between his fingertips. "Where have you been? Why didn't I see you on the
way here?"

She pulled her face away. "None of your business."

He immediately knew that demands would get him nowhere. Anger had given Charlotte the confidence she'd
previously lacked around him. Yet this stubborn woman enticed him even more. "I worried for you."

Her eyes softened, exposing the gentle heart of her.
"You shouldn't have. I went downtown to do some shop-

ping. You probably didn't see me coming home because I walked through the vineyard instead of using the lane."

"In the dark? You walked, what is the distance—" he frowned in thought "—more than two miles in the dark?"

"I know this land like the back of my hand and it's barely two miles, not over two miles."

He wasn't appeased. "Charlotte, if I were not a patient man, I would be inclined to be very harsh with you for taking such a chance. You know nothing about the temporary workers who may be about." He fought the surge of protectiveness that he had no right to display. Gritting his teeth, he told himself that that would soon be rectified. Then he could look after her as she was meant to be looked after.

"Who said you're a patient man?" Charlotte muttered.

Her feminine temper seemed to have thawed under his concern and when he laced the fingers of one hand through hers, she didn't immediately move to tug them away. He imagined he could feel the quickening beat of her heart through their linked hands.

"I have the patience of a saint," he said, tongue in cheek. "Else I would give up trying to coax you and just kidnap you to my chalet deep in the Swiss mountains."

Fascination glimmered in her eyes.

Leaning over until their lips almost touched, he whispered, "Once I had you all to myself, I would do things to you that would make your toes curl." When her breath caught, he continued, "That kiss was of very great moment—you know that and so do I. Forgive me for trying to lessen it. Come, *chérie,* don't be angry with me."

Alexandre's silkily seductive voice rubbed along Charlotte's nerve endings, setting them afire. It was a potent weapon of seduction, designed to reduce a woman to nothing more than a sensate being, greedy and needy. For a moment, her body swayed toward him.

She believed him about the value of the single kiss
they'd shared. She understood why he'd come looking for
her when they'd barely met. She understood why he felt
he had the right to demand her business, why his maleness
sought to brand her with his mark.

That kiss had been far more than anything so simple as
a kiss. It had been a claiming and the shocking thing was,
it had been in no way one-sided. Barely a breath from his
lips, she made the mistake of looking into those dark, enigmatic eyes. There was such hunger there, such possession,
such *need*.

Fear spiked.

With a painful start she realized that she could never be
enough for this magnificent man. Alexandre needed a
woman supremely confident of her own sexuality, her own
feminine appeal, a woman ready to accept the invitation in
his eyes and partner him in the most intimate of dances.
Charlotte wasn't even close.

Her body froze. "Please," she whispered, unable to hide
the ache inside her. "Please go."

Stay, her heart whispered. *Stay,* her body moaned. *Stay.*
But of course, she couldn't say that. Only in her dreams
could she captivate a man like Alexandre and fulfill the sensual demands he would make of her as his woman.

"Charlotte." His fingers refused to release hers. "Do
you really believe that I'm a man who hurts women?"

It was the moment's vulnerability in his tone that got to
her. "No. You…you tempt women."

"Let me tempt you." His voice alone was temptation
enough, the heat in his eyes pure sorcery.

Fighting the sensual pull between them with everything
she had, she tugged away her hand and tried to close the
door. "I'm sorry but this can't happen." With every word
she spoke, she felt more and more the coward. The urge to

tell him that what she already felt for him scared her, was almost overwhelming.

"Why not?" He blocked the doorway, big and proud.

Swallowing, she said, "You can't give me what I need. You can't be the man I need." What she needed from a man was a kind of surrender that strong, dominant Alexandre Dupree would never agree to. And even if he did, she'd still be left with her inadequacies.

His darkly beautiful face was suddenly a mask. "You've made yourself very clear. I'm sorry I bothered you." He stepped back, that lithely muscled body held fiercely in check. "Lock the door."

This time, she didn't argue. Maybe she was a coward, but was it cowardice to want to avoid humiliation of the kind which would result when Alexandre realized she wasn't woman enough for him?

Alexandre pulled out of the Ashton Estate in his rental car, a low-slung black Ferrari, a sleek and powerful machine. Instead of letting frustration take him on an aimless drive, he headed toward San Pablo Bay.

Charlotte had asked him to leave. Had told him that he "couldn't be the man" she needed. A woman couldn't find a much clearer way to reject a man—it felt like she'd reached into his body and clawed his heart, an emotional mauling he could barely comprehend.

For the first time in his life, his shield of emotional distance had not only cracked, it had broken into pieces. *And he hadn't even been aware of it happening.*

How had one small woman come to mean so much to him in so short a time? Even after her blunt rebuff, he craved her. Until now, he'd sincerely believed that the attraction he felt wasn't one-sided. Obviously, he'd been fooling himself, something he despised.

Ever since he'd been a child, truth had been the most important thing in his life because he'd been asked to tell lies from too early an age. They may have been lies of omission, but they'd marked him. He'd never allowed himself the comfort of falseness.

Shifting gears, he rose up an incline. How could she not feel the fire that burned him every time he thought of her, of those big brown eyes so full of passion and so unawakened? He hated the thought that some other man would be the one to awaken the slumbering sensuality he sensed in her, hated it in a way that made a mockery of anything he'd ever before felt for a woman.

His eye landed on the speedometer as he turned a corner. He swore sharply and reduced his dangerous speed. It was tempting to keep pushing the machine to the limit, but he knew he'd never forgive himself if he caused someone else an injury because he was in a temper. Ruling out a long drive, he searched for a place to stop and calm down.

A few minutes later, he noticed a small hill. Cruising up, he parked but left the engine running. Unclipping his safety belt, he opened the door and walked out to stand in the cool night air. When he went to put his hands in his pants pockets, he frowned. Something was weighing down one side of his jacket. Reaching into a pocket, he pulled out a slim volume.

The scent of Charlotte rose from the book—frangipani and moonlight. Gut clenching, he moved into the light thrown by the car's headlights and flipped open the book, curious as to what Charlotte wrote about her plants. In all honesty, he felt compelled to learn everything he could about this woman who haunted him.

All these years, women had come easily to him but he'd never taken them for granted, well aware of their fickle nature. Not letting one of them become too important to him had been a simple matter. Yet, somehow, Charlotte was making him break those rules. And the irony was, she didn't want him at all.

The first page was filled with writing characterized by curves and roundness, displaying the writer's inherently giving nature. He found himself tracing the words with his fingers, as if he could feel Charlotte. Unable to read what they said in the low-slung lights, he moved into the car and flicked on the overhead switch.

Lover Mine,

The words slammed into him like a two arm punch. If he'd still been standing, he might've doubled over. His sweet, innocent Charlotte had a lover? A lover she wrote letters to? Was this her copy of those letters?

He knew he should stop reading, but couldn't—not when the possessive beast inside him was growling in outrage. In less than two days, she'd become *his* and he didn't share.

Lover Mine,
Will you be gentle with me the first time we make love? Will you be tender? Will you understand that for me, this act is more than bodies meeting, more than simple pleasure, more than just the physical?

I'd never lie with you if I didn't adore you.

Do I love you? I've seen so much pain and betrayal in this family—I'm not even sure I know what love is. But, I do know that for me to lie with you means that I care…deeply.

Fists clenched, Alexandre checked the date of the entry. Almost six months ago. Surely Charlotte and her lover had consummated their relationship by now. He turned the page.

Lover Mine,

I've always been a good girl.

Except in my fantasies. Of course you know that. How could you not? You know that in those fantasies, I'm another person, another Charlotte, one who's wild and wicked and just a little bit dangerous. In my fantasies, I do things that I can't speak of in the daylight or even in the moonlight.

In my fantasies, I'm a woman of bone-deep sensuality, as alluring and enticing as the Sirens of old, a woman who draws men not to their doom...but to their absolute pleasure.

There was nothing overtly sexual about her words, but his arousal pounded low and deep. The last words lingered on his retinas, as if burned on them.

Once more, he accepted that he was invading her privacy in a way he could never justify, that he should stop. But the need to brand the unpalatable truth into his soul compelled him to continue.

The truth that Charlotte belonged to another man.

Jealousy shot through his nerve endings—who the hell had dared touch her? Touch the only woman who'd succeeded in reaching Alexandre's long jaded soul, succeeded in waking him up to passion again. Reaching out a tanned hand, he flipped the page.

Sometimes, I wonder what it would be like to give you such complete trust that I'd do anything you asked, without question...without hesitation. I can almost see you, lover mine—see your strength, your searing sexuality, your dominant tendencies.

In my fantasies, you're strong enough to treat my submission as the gift it is, to give me commands

laced with rough tenderness, to openly adore my
body without seeing it as a weakness. And, you're
strong enough to understand and accept that by doing what I ask, you have surrendered to me and my
desires.

I've never met a man capable of fulfilling this
most sinful fantasy. Will you be the only lover I ever know?

Alexandre felt understanding start to awaken, but it
remained tantalizingly out of reach, buried under jealousy such as he'd never thought himself capable of. Unable to bear reading more about Charlotte's sexual
awakening with another man, he almost shut the book,
but some inexplicable need made him flip through to the
last entry.

He had to know—had he made any impact on her? Or
had he been nothing to her, adoring as she was of this lover of hers. He opened the page to an entry dated two days
ago, the day they'd met.

Lover mine,
Until today, you've never had a face…

Alexandre's eyes widened.

…never had a name. You've just been the lover I
needed in every way. You were my creation so I could
shape you, mold you, delete the parts of you that I
didn't like. You were my ultimate fantasy, a man created for me alone, a man for whom my pleasure was
his only goal and my cries as I shattered under his
loving reward enough.

"Of course it would be, *ma chérie*," Alexandre murmured, "why would you think otherwise?"

But today, you suddenly have a face and a voice. You could seduce me with that slow, seductive accent alone. I can imagine you whispering to me as we lie tangled in the most intimate of embraces, that voice of yours rippling along my spine, turning my insides to hot honey.

Alexandre felt excitement begin to flicker through his nerves. Surely he couldn't be mistaken as to whose voice gave Charlotte such erotic pleasure? That would be far too cruel. Taking a deep breath, he read on.

And then I look up into your eyes and I'm lost, utterly yours. You're so tempting, so seductive, so masculinely beautiful that you take my breath away. I know I can't be the woman you need but I ache to try.

When you look at me with heat in your eyes, I can almost believe that I'm the woman you think me to be. I can almost be the woman I fantasize about being, a woman who embraces passion without fear.

Tenderness gripped him, tight and powerful. It shocked him that Charlotte was unsure of her lovely sensuality when she had no reason to be.

Even now, I hesitate to write your name for fear that I'll tempt the Fates and they'll take even the fleeting pleasure of your presence from me. I long to see you, touch you, listen to you.

And yet when you come near, I can't help but run,

for part of me recognizes the hunter in you. I'm not sure I'm ready to be your prey…Alexandre.

His breath punched out of him as adrenaline rushed through every pore. Sweat trickled down his spine. Who would've guessed that his prim and proper Charlotte had such heated fantasies?

Even more shocking was the urgent desire he had to fulfill each and every one of them, in any way she chose. Control came easily to him. It would be no hardship to play her games in bed, even to give her the surrender she needed. The gift of her trust would be compensation enough. But would she give him that gift?

In her fantasies, he was the lover she ached for. But, as she'd written, when he came near her in reality, she ran. Tonight, she'd backed away from him so completely that had he not read this journal, he would've believed that she felt nothing for him.

Why such a difference between reality and fantasy? Frowning, he decided he'd have to read the whole journal. Perhaps a gentleman might've returned it without perusing the rest of its contents, but when it came to Charlotte, Alexandre found he was no gentleman.

The autocratic tyrant in him had finally woken up after years of silence, and he was intent on claiming and branding sweet Charlotte Ashton as his very own. Any worries Alexandre might've harbored about the chains of commitment and desire, crumbled under the force of the hunger and possessiveness raging through him.

Four

Charlotte was frantic. She couldn't find her journal. She'd turned the cottage upside down without success. Panic had her almost hyperventilating. What if someone read what she'd written?

Suddenly, like a ray of light on a cloudy day, she remembered scribbling in it madly the night after Alexandre's first visit to the greenhouse. Breath whooshing out of her, she ran to the greenhouse…only to come to a skidding halt. Her gaze fell on the long, muscular form of the male who'd spent the night tormenting her in her dreams, lounging against a glass wall.

"You are in a hurry, Charlotte."

Her eyes couldn't look away from the inherent sensuality of his mouth. She swallowed. Hard. "I need to check something in my, um, gardening journal."

His eyes glinted for a moment, but then those sinful lips

curved into a smile. "Of course." Reaching out, he pushed open the door.

Unable to avoid it, she ducked under his arm and walked inside. She found her journal exactly where she remembered leaving it. Alexandre prowled in behind her. She thanked God he hadn't come in earlier. What if he'd read the things she'd written? Her face flushed. He'd probably have laughed his head off at her fantasies, at the things she believed herself capable of when it was only dreams and not reality.

"Did you want something?" She turned, aware her voice had become husky and soft.

As always, his presence shattered the calm she'd worked so hard to achieve, the peace she'd tried to create in this world where she didn't quite fit in. Despite that, her eyes drank in the sight of him, her traitorous body sighing with relief.

He hadn't walked away as she'd asked him to do, something she'd spent the night dreading. Her inability to stick to her decision to keep him at a distance unsettled her, but what terrified her was that no man had ever compared to her fantasy lover. No man but Alexandre Dupree.

"Yes, I have a commission for you." Dressed in sand-colored slacks teamed with a simple white shirt, he looked very elegant, very worldly. And yet, he didn't seem the least out of place in her haven of jungle-wild plants and delicate rosebuds, as if he were some wild, elemental creature himself.

It took a moment for his words to penetrate. "A commission? Are you throwing a party?" Even as she spoke, she was reaching for the pad in the back pocket of her jeans, her hand pulling out the pen clipped to the spine. She placed her journal on the workbench.

"Why don't you write in your gardening notebook?" Alexandre's eyes were suspiciously blank, his tone as smooth as melted caramel.

For a moment, she froze, wondering if he'd read her fantasies after all. Then he blinked and the impression was gone, leaving her feeling paranoid. "It's…um, for the notations about the plants, not commissions. So, what did you want and when?" Well aware of the possible double entrende in her last sentence, she waited for him to tease her with a little sensual byplay, as he'd done in the vineyard.

"I need a single arrangement, for a private gift." There was nothing but business in his tone. "By tonight. I'm prepared to pay double your usual fee for the short notice." He had his checkbook in his hands.

She looked up, a sinking feeling in the pit of her stomach. "I don't do private arrangements."

"For a friend of the family, surely you can make an exception?"

Charlotte was shocked by the calm question. Not an ounce of the charm he'd been dosing her with so liberally for the past two days was visible. It was apparent that he'd taken her back-off signal very seriously. There would be no more sensual overtures from this wild wolf of a man who'd been stalking her.

"Tonight?" she asked, trying to fight her overwhelming sense of loss. How could he have become so important to her in mere days? "I have so much work."

"Please? It's very important." His voice was rich chocolate, sinful and tempting.

Her resistance to him was nil. "All right. Is it for a business associate, a friend…?"

"A lover," he said softly.

Her back stiffened, but she could hardly refuse the request now that she'd accepted. It would betray too much. "You want roses?" A bouquet of roses would be easy enough to prepare, she thought, trying to submerge her sudden hurt in a flood of practicality.

"*Non,* roses are too common for one such as she. I want

something unique, beautiful, elegant and utterly lovely, just like her."

A surge of jealousy almost overwhelmed Charlotte. She wanted to slap his handsome face. All this time he'd been flirting with her, charming her, when he'd had a lover tucked away, a lover who was everything she wasn't.

"The arrangement must be alluring, but not overpowering." Alexandre's dark eyes gentled. "She is a bud of perfect beauty and my gift must show that I understand her need to go slow, to take pleasure in every moment of her awakening. It must convey my apology for pushing her too fast, rushing her in my desire for her."

Charlotte was clutching her pen so hard, she thought she might break it. There was no need to write down a single word. Every syllable was emblazoned into her brain. "Come back at seven." The words were clipped.

There was just so much she could take. Right now, she wanted to throw something at him. She'd give him his arrangement all right—she'd give him something so perfectly awful that his lover would never even speak to him again.

But when she finally forced herself to work on the creation, she made it delicate and beautiful, fragrant but not too lush—colored for freshness in creamy white and golden yellow, with the merest hints of red for passion. For Alexandre's lover would have passion. Otherwise, he wouldn't have spoken of her with such intense hunger.

Because his lover was unique, she used rare hothouse orchids in shades of gold, offsetting their sophistication with white pansies so delicate they'd bruise if stroked too hard, for Alexandre's lover required gentle handling. To add the touch of red, the touch of passion, she used leaves; tiny, perfectly shaped leaves of such vibrant beauty that they were almost flowers in themselves.

The centerpiece was, of course, a pure white rosebud of

perfect beauty, carefully hidden amongst the confident orchids, shy but compelling the eye to look its way.

And then it was finished.

She felt a moment of complete joy. This was her art and she was good at what she did. A second later, her happiness crumbled as she realized that this arrangement was one she would've died to receive herself. All those instructions that Alexandre had given her, they were too much like the woman she wanted to be.

Looking at her watch, she saw that it was close to seven. She'd spent hours longer on this piece than she should have. But at least she had the satisfaction of knowing that Alexandre had paid through the nose. It was too little to compensate her for her pain, but she focused on it in an effort to control her emotions.

A soft footfall sounded behind her. Without turning, she said, "It's done."

Coming to stand just behind her, Alexandre reached out to touch a pansy with exquisite care. "You're truly talented, *ma petite.*"

"Don't call me that," she snapped. The way he said it, it was an endearment, a lover's caress, and she knew she was no lover of his.

"As you wish." There was a smile in his voice.

But when she turned, his eyes were solemn. "I'm sure she'll treasure it. Thank you, Charlotte."

And just that quickly, he was gone, taking her creation. For another woman.

As had happened the night before, the phone rang just as she was stepping out of the shower. Dressed only in a big towel tucked haphazardly around her, her hair piled up on her head out of the way, she grabbed the receiver. "Charlotte speaking."

"You sound breathless. What have you been doing?" Amusement lingered in the seduction of Alexandre's voice.

She almost answered him, caught by the undertone of command. "Is something wrong with the arrangement?" she forced herself to ask.

"*Non.* It's perfect. I called to say that I left you something of a thank-you gift."

"There was no need," she began, painfully aware that nothing would make up for the hollow feeling in her stomach. With her own words, she'd destroyed whatever might've grown between them. The quickness with which he'd moved on to another woman should've had her thanking her lucky stars. Then why did she want to cry?

"There was every need," he said, his voice that low purr that always made her want to curl into his lap and rub herself against his body. "It's on the doorstep. I hope you like it." He hung up.

Charlotte stood for a second, debating whether to go and see what he'd left her. More than likely, it was a bottle of wine or chocolates, she thought, indulging her need to sulk.

He'd probably put no more thought into her gift than he would for any other employee. After all, she wasn't a lover whose flowers had to be perfect, had to show that he thought her *unique, beautiful, elegant and utterly lovely.*

In the end, her curiosity got the better of her. She headed toward the door, uncaring of her state of undress. After all, who was going to see her way out here? Pulling open the door, she looked down. Her eyes widened. Tremors shivered through her entire body, starting from her heart and traveling through every nerve she possessed.

Disbelieving, she went to her knees. Hardly daring to touch what she'd handled so easily earlier, she reached out and stroked the silky soft petal of a tiny white blossom so beautifully perfect, it was almost impossibly real.

What had he said?

She is a bud of perfect beauty...

A single tear rolled down her face.

...my gift must show that I understand her need to go slow, to take pleasure in every moment of her awakening. It must convey my apology for pushing her too fast, rushing her in my desire for her.

"Ah, Charlotte, this was to make you smile, not cry." Sounding like he couldn't bear to see her tears, Alexandre was suddenly crouching on the other side of the flowers, wiping them away.

She should've been startled at his appearance, but she wasn't. Not when her body had known all along that he was nearby. She tried to speak but couldn't, shaking her head instead and reproaching him with her eyes. In the space of a single day, he'd shattered her heart and rebuilt it with a fatal flaw. And that flaw was him.

"I'm sorry, *chérie.* I thought you'd like them." He sounded so genuinely distressed that she began to smile. She'd never thought to see cool, elegant Alexandre Dupree out of his element.

"They're perfect," she repeated his judgment. "But you're an impossible man."

"So does this mean you are *ma petite* again?" That charming smile blazed back to life.

She didn't point out that she'd never agreed to be any such thing. The light in his eyes was too entrancing to dim. She had the feeling that despite his easy charm, Alexandre rarely smiled with such simple delight.

At that moment, he touched her cheek. "Will you not return inside? You must be cold."

Startled, she looked down at herself—to her intense relief the towel had stayed put. Holding the bouquet protectively in her arms, she rose and backed into the house. "You can come in."

Every nerve in her body went wild with warning. If she let this wild wolf into her house, he'd corner her until she was completely at his mercy. The thing of it was, she didn't want to resist.

To her surprise, he shook his head. "You make me forget my vows when you stand there looking so very lovely. I meant what I said. I won't rush you. But, I'm man enough to ask you for a kiss—I'm not quite sure you've forgiven me."

She realized he didn't intend to come to her and claim his kiss. He truly was *asking*. Swallowing, she put his gift on the nearby coffee table. Then, heart thudding, she took two steps toward him.

His smile died. "Am I so distasteful to you, *chérie,* that you must screw up your courage to kiss me? If that is so, I withdraw my request. Hurting you is the last thing I wish to do."

Charlotte found herself almost running to him. "How can you think that?" she asked, pained at the bleakness in his eyes. "I…I'm just not…good at this," she admitted. "Help me." It was the first time in a long, long time that she'd asked anyone for help.

Alexandre felt his sophistication shatter under her whispered words. Tenderness that was almost savage in its intensity took hold of him, the passion in him merging with protectiveness such as he'd never before felt. Reaching out, he touched one golden cheek, stunned that a woman with her sensual nature would be so unaware of the sway she held over him.

"Charlotte," he whispered, sliding his hand slowly around her nape. He tugged gently, until she was standing on the edge of the doorway, while he remained outside.

"You smell delicious—can I have you for dessert?"

She responded as he'd hoped, her nervousness buried under amusement. "Stop misbehaving."

He felt a smile light his eyes at her mock-stern expression. "Your wish is my command." On her nape, he moved his thumb, stroking the softness of her skin, the sheer temptation of her. *"Tu es très belle."* Bending his head, he touched petal-soft lips as alluring as any one of her fragrant blooms.

At first, she was still. When he continued to barely brush their lips together in the most gentle of seductions, her body softened and her lips parted on a breath. Moving the hand curved around her nape to the golden skin bared above the towel, he rubbed his thumb along the dip of her collarbone. She gasped, her mouth opening fully under his. Then she finally touched him, pressing those fine, competent hands against his chest.

The urge to crush her sweetly welcoming body against his was almost inescapable—he fought it because he did indeed intend to savor and relish every moment of her awakening. However, he accepted the invitation of her lips, the well-hidden primitive in him starving for a taste of her lush sensuality.

Her soft moan caught him unawares. His hand tightened on her shoulder for the barest fraction of a second before he forced himself to release her, breaking the kiss before he broke his promise. The newly awakened possessiveness flaring through him wanted nothing more than to rip that towel from her body and indulge.

Her lashes lifted and liquid dark eyes met his, half-shocked, half-delighted. "I never knew a kiss could be like that."

"Neither did I." It was no lie. He'd never been so affected by a simple kiss, so hungry that he was hard and ready, more than willing to take any invitation she offered. It disturbed him, the power she had over his body, but not enough to make him stop his pursuit.

"Go to sleep, *ma petite*. Dream of me." Meant to be a tease, it came out an order. He decided he liked giving her that order, particularly when her eyes widened even further.

"Alexandre, you…" She just shook her head and stepped back into her fairy-tale cottage, the princess retreating from the marauder at her door. Just when he thought she'd close it, she smiled just the tiniest bit and said, "Unique, beautiful, elegant and utterly lovely?"

Leaning forward, he picked up her hand and brought it to his lips, placing the softest of kisses on the tender skin of her inner wrist. "I forgot to add something."

"What?" It was a breathy question, her pulse jumping under his touch.

He released her before she seduced him absolutely. Stepping back into the shadows, he allowed himself a smile at having finally breached her defenses. "Luscious."

Five

Long after Alexandre had prowled off into the darkness, Charlotte sat wide-awake. She kept touching the flowers, smiling for no reason and then shivering. Not in cold. Not in fear. In desire.

Luscious.

That divinely sexy man thought she was luscious. She knew she shouldn't believe him, not when he had that dangerous charm. He probably said things like that all the time to get women into his bed. Of course he probably didn't have to try very hard. A man that tempting could seduce with nothing more than a glance.

Did she want to be seduced into his bed?

Charlotte gulped and stroked a glossy red leaf, accepting the truth. Since the moment she'd seen him, *want* had become her constant companion. Her hands fluttered to lips still throbbing from the barely restrained passion of Alexandre's kiss. Hunger had thrummed through that lithely muscular frame, but he'd kept it under rigid control, giving her the tenderness she needed. She wondered if he'd be just as tender in every other step of their dance.

Could she take a chance on him?

Her wariness of rich, sophisticated men rose from her knowledge that sometimes, the core of them was rotten. Witnessing Spencer manipulate Lilah all these years had left her with a healthy disrespect for the type. Yet, something defied her to think of Alexandre in the same breath as Spencer.

Her hands clenched and frown lines marred her brow. She wanted Alexandre but to her, the sharing of bodies was special, a gift to be cherished. It wasn't something she'd ever take lightly. Then again, what she felt for Alexandre was in no way light or easy.

He made her feel fiercely female, a sensual being who hungered to learn of passion and heat. More than that, he made her feel proud of herself, of her worth as a woman. When he looked at her, he saw beauty.

Luscious.

Blushing, Charlotte finally made her way to bed, sliding in between the cool sheets dressed only in her skin. It was one of her secret indulgences, a concession to the sensual core of her, a core that most people would never see. As the sheets whispered over her heated skin, she couldn't help remembering Alexandre's command.

Dream of me.

He needn't have given the order. She'd been doing that since the moment she'd laid eyes on him.

The next day, Charlotte rose before dawn to put the finishing touches on several completed arrangements, her mind on a man with dark chocolate eyes. A shiver ran through her at the memory of those eyes full of barely controlled hunger. What would it be like to have all that hunger focused on her? Could she cope?

Shaking her head, she sprayed some flowers with water and fiddled with the placement of a spray of baby's breath. The arrangements were for the reception that would follow a wedding taking place on the grounds today. The only thing she had to prepare for the wedding itself was a floral arbor, leafy vines and delicate white roses twisting around a metal frame. She planned to do that on the spot, before she organized the arrangements in the reception hall.

The sound of a golf cart arriving interrupted her fussing. Smiling, she walked out and supervised the loading of her precious flowers onto the three carts that had turned up, driven by staff Megan had hired to help with the wedding. She caught a ride up with the flowers, having the men drop her off at the winery with her roses and vines.

The arbor's frame was already in place to the side of the winery, where the actual wedding would be taking place. After sending the drivers to the estate house with strict instructions to place her arrangements gently on a couple of the tables, she spent the next hour and a half on the arbor. Once complete, it nicely complemented the crushed lengths of white silk that marked out the aisle in lieu of ropes.

Megan walked over from where she'd been overseeing the placement of chairs. "Didn't want to interrupt you while you looked so serious," she teased.

Charlotte smiled. Megan had definitely mellowed since her marriage to Simon—she seemed far more at ease with herself these days. "What do you think?"

"Gorgeous as always. I wish I had your artistic ability."

"I'll leave you to it. I have to set up the flowers for the reception."

"At least with you, I know the work will be superb. It's the other idiots I have to worry about."

Laughing, Charlotte hitched a ride on one of the carts going back and forth from the estate house to the winery grounds. As she ran up the four steps into a house which had always intimidated her, she kept an eye out for Alexandre. However, he didn't make an appearance.

Feeling oddly deflated when she finished at around 10:00 a.m., she hopped on her bike, having had it brought up on one of the carts. A sleek black Ferrari purred down the estate drive as she was about to take off.

Curious about the occupant, she took her time pushing off her kickstand and arranging her small backpack. Though she wasn't a woman impressed by material possessions, she was human enough to appreciate the sleek lines of a car that looked like a crouching hunting cat.

To her surprise, the car changed direction and circled around the reflecting pool to head straight for her, stopping inches from her bike. Scowling, she wondered if she'd have to fend off the advances of some playboy guest who'd arrived early.

Then the door opened and a man who looked even more like a predator than his car, stepped out. "*Ma chérie,* do not tell me you have been here all morning?"

"Yes, setting up for the Harrington wedding." She wanted to ask him where he'd been but her throat closed up as he neared her, his big hands going to her own. Startled, she let him pick them up, balancing herself using her feet.

"You're scratched," he accused.

She laughed. "Happens all the time. Flowers are pretty but they do occasionally have thorns."

"Take better care of yourself." It was a command.

"Alexandre," she began, intending on telling him to stop with the orders. After the way he'd kissed her so tenderly last night, after the precious words he'd given her, she was no longer tongue-tied in his presence. This man wanted to hear what she had to say.

Lifting her hand to his lips, he kissed one long, angry scratch. "I like that." He began to nibble teasingly on her knuckles.

She wanted to moan. "What?"

"My name on your lips." The way he was staring at those lips made her want to go up in flames.

"I have to go." She didn't know why she'd said that, when she'd planned this day off weeks in advance. Maybe she wasn't completely over being tongue-tied in his presence.

"Do you have time for dinner with me, Charlotte?" He was all sexy male appeal, deep masculine dimples creasing his cheeks.

Her heart melted. "You're too charming for your own good."

He didn't laugh as she expected. Instead, that coaxing smile faded. "Charm is not all I am."

The fleeting darkness in his eyes took her mind back to their other meetings. Alexandre, she realized, always kept a distance between himself and the rest of the world. He was so charming, she didn't think most people ever noticed that he never revealed his emotions.

But she'd noticed because she was the same. She didn't trust easily. Walker was the only person who was close to her. She adored her elder brother despite her concern about his loyalty to a man like Spencer, but even he didn't know her innermost thoughts and feelings.

Knowing how alone it could feel to hurt inside where no one could see, she ached to soothe the scars hidden beneath Alexandre's sophisticated elegance. Would he ever trust her enough to share his secrets?

Would she one day trust him enough to share her own?

"Dinner? Yes, I'm free," she found herself saying, taking a chance on this man who'd so suddenly, so quickly, touched her in the most well-guarded part of herself.

"I'll come by for you at nine." He released her hands, which he'd been gently stroking the whole time they'd been talking, creating havoc with her senses.

Her eyes widened. "Isn't that a bit late?"

He grimaced. "I'll be closeted with your winemaking staff and then with Trace. Can you wait?"

That he wanted her company that much was something she couldn't resist. "I'll ride up here to meet you."

"It will be dark." His brows gathered.

"It's safe." Watching Lilah had taught Charlotte that women who let men have all the say in a relationship ended up doormats. No matter how beautiful and pampered a life she lived, Lilah was Spencer's puppet. When he jerked, she moved. "I'll meet you by your car at nine."

Still scowling, he muttered something dark in French. "Yes, I think my *maman* would like you very much, *ma petite*."

She wondered what he meant by that. "You're very busy."

"Never too busy for you." A small smile flirting with his lips, he laid a final kiss on the pulse of her wrist. "Until tonight, my lovely, luscious Charlotte." He grinned at her uncontrollable blush. "Definitely luscious."

Alexandre watched Charlotte ride off, his eyes on her sweet body but his mind on her dreams.

Lover Mine,

Do you know what I'd like tonight?

I'd like to be taken on a picnic in the moonlight, under the spreading branches of some majestic tree. I'd like to be treated like a treasure—adored with

your eyes, seduced by your flattery, kissed by the
touch of your fingers on mine.

I want you to take my hand and dance with me to
the music of the leaves in the swaying trees, not a
word said between us that isn't a murmur of desire,
a temptation of the senses.

But, nothing more.

I want you to give me this moment of romance
without asking for anything physical in return. Just
my company. And my smile.

Alexandre smiled throughout the day, accompanied
by thoughts of Charlotte. She believed that her longing
for romance would be a hardship for a man. In truth,
charming her in the moonlight would be his distinct
pleasure.

Some men didn't understand the value of loveplay, the
delight that came from romancing the woman you adored.
Alexandre had never been that kind of man. Not even as a
youth had he rushed.

He'd always known that seducing a woman's body
wasn't enough. A good lover gave just as much attention
to his woman's mind, her heart and her soul. He'd always
known that but never before had he paid it such heed.

This time, he meant to charm absolutely, to adore without reservation. With her secrets hidden behind midnight
eyes and that deep core of sensuality, Charlotte appealed
to the carefully controlled savage inside of him. And that
part of him wanted everything from her when they took the
final steps of this intimate dance. Passion and heat, lust and
surrender, trust and desire.

Such trust in bed was the most precious of gifts. Even
more so when the woman giving it didn't do so lightly. If
Charlotte chose to share her body with him, it would mean

far more than a moment's fleeting pleasure, far more than anything he'd ever before experienced.

That night when he met Charlotte by the car, he satisfied himself with a kiss on her cheek and then opened the door. Dressed in a long denim skirt with ruffles of white lace at the bottom, and a silky white blouse that looked as soft as moonlight, she took his breath away.

As they drove out of the estate, he glanced at the shimmering beauty of her. "You look like an exotic temptation."

Her laugh was intimate in the darkness inside the car. "Have you kidnapped me?"

He turned carefully onto the road, mindful of the treasure he carried this night. "*Oui,* of course. I'm taking you to my secret hideout where I shall ravish you." The words were playful, but the images in his mind went far beyond mere play.

"Where *are* you taking me?" There was a smile in her question.

"That's a surprise."

"You've got me turned around already." She looked out at the narrow side road he'd pulled into.

"Good." He wanted to kiss that curious little nose.

"Are you sure you know where you're going?"

"I'm very sure." But, was he?

In the past, carrying on a discreet affair had never been a problem. He'd chosen his partners for the same reason they'd sought him out—neither side wanted the demands of commitment. When it was time to let go, they did so with grace and a smile. Several of his old lovers counted him as a close friend.

With Charlotte, the rules were different—*he* was different. He wanted to cage her in his arms and keep her for himself, to enjoy and adore whenever he wished. His feelings for her already bordered on dangerous possessiveness.

His mind sensed the threat—for the first time in his life, a woman might just seduce him to addiction. It was something he'd fought against for a lifetime, schooled by his childhood to expect nothing from women but their fleeting company.

Never loyalty. Never forever.

And yet, he couldn't walk away from this dance.

"Alexandre." Charlotte's voice whispered over his body like a sweet caress.

His arousal was swift and almost painful. *"Oui, ma petite?"*

"You just went so quiet," she said, gentle in her question. "Is everything all right?"

Her care touched a part of him that nothing had touched for a long time, somehow managing to soothe the raging beast of passion into something more controllable. "Everything is as it should be."

She made a sound of frustration. "You're very good at answering questions without giving anything away."

He admired her spirit. "Perhaps you're not asking the right questions." He'd never given a woman that entrée, that chance to find the right question to ask.

"Will you answer me if I ask the right one?"

"It depends on my mood," he teased. "If you've seduced me into submission, then I shall be at your mercy. I suggest you question me in bed."

"Alexandre!"

He chuckled at her scandalized response, the painful knot inside him unraveling in the light of her presence. At the same time, a startling thought shimmered into being. Could this tiny woman help him find a way out of the darkness of his past? A past shaped by deception and shame—he loved his *maman,* but the lessons he'd learned at her knee were not something he'd wish on any child.

They'd scarred him and he was intelligent enough to know that he was the man he was because of those invisible wounds. A man who cherished women but never enough to place his faith in them, never enough to chance his heart. Even as a child, he'd been comfortable relying only on himself, but this aloneness was of the soul.

Until Charlotte, no woman had ever come close to breaching that wall of scar tissue. But what right did he have to taint her with the dishonor of his past? She was as dew-fresh as a morning flower—what good would it do to sully her dreams of love and loyalty?

Seeing a landmark up ahead, he took a deep breath and forced the unexpected tumble of questions aside. Tonight was for her. And, he realized with surprise, for him. That savage primitive in him was intrigued by the idea of romance under the moonlight with this lovely woman. "Look ahead, my innocent little Charlotte."

"Stop it, you… oh. It looks like a—meadow. How did you find this?" Her eyes roved over the rolling patch of spring green grass silvered by the moonlight.

"I'm a sorcerer, *chérie*. I know many things."

Charlotte couldn't believe the beauty outside the window. Dotted with spring flowers that nodded sleepily in the night, the area appeared enchanted. Several large trees curved around the grassy field, and in the distance she could see fairy mist rising, lending a soft intimacy to the night. It was like something out of a dream. Her dream. As soon as the car stopped, she unclipped her belt, intent on getting out.

"Wait, let me care for you."

Startled, she watched him get out and walk over to open the door. Delighted at the unexpected chivalry, she stepped out. "Nobody does that anymore."

Closing her door, he took one of her hands in his. "You deserve it, Charlotte."

She loved the way he said her name, as if it were something exotic when it was so very ordinary. "I always wanted a Lakota Sioux name," she said, surprising herself with the confidence. "My mother's name was Mary Little Dove—isn't that the most beautiful name you ever heard?"

He tipped his head to the side. "Is that your heritage? The Sioux?"

"My mother was Oglala Lakota Sioux." Walker had told her that when she'd asked him why they looked so different from the other Ashtons. He'd already been pulling away from her by then, distancing himself from the tragedy of their past, but had loved her enough to try and soothe her confusion.

"I'm afraid I don't know much about them."

Her smile was weak. "Neither do I. I was raised with my cousins. I suppose nobody thought it was important to teach me about my mother's people."

"But you miss not knowing half of yourself."

There was a depth of knowledge in his answer that made her heart flood with tenderness. Then and there, her resolve to breach his reserve and discover what haunted him, firmed into a vow.

She knew instinctively that he was a man used to looking after his women. He'd already given her so much— made her feel precious and wanted. Well, she decided, this woman was going to return the favor. But, she let it go for now, aware it would take time. "Yes."

He curved his arms around her waist, as if to shelter her from the night. "Perhaps you should seek out your heritage?"

Trusting the wrong man could lead to shattering pain, but she was tired of the aloneness of her search. And there was a seductive core of honor about Alexandre that made her want to place her faith in him. "I've heard that they're very protective of themselves, that it's hard to gain their trust. What if…what if they don't want to talk to me?"

Alexandre frowned. "How can they deny you when you are one of them?

"But that's just it. I don't belong with the Sioux, just like I don't belong on the estate. I'm an in-between person, someone who fits nowhere." She stopped, dismayed at the depth of hurt she'd betrayed. "I'm sorry…"

"Never be sorry for trusting me." Alexandre cupped her face with one hand and brushed her lips with his undeniably male mouth. It was a gesture of tenderness and it shook her. "Perhaps instead of feeling as if you don't belong in either world, you should think instead that you're lucky to have two worlds?"

Touched, she returned the simple but powerful caress. "I'll think about it. But not tonight. Tonight is for us."

His dark eyes gleamed but he acquiesced to her request. "Let me retrieve the picnic basket and blanket."

As they walked across the field to the moon-shadow of a large tree, Alexandre pondered over Charlotte's revelation. She and her flowers were so much a part of the Ashton Estate, he'd never considered that she might not feel as if she fit in. And yet, once he thought about it, he could see how she was different. Unique.

It wasn't only her looks, though they were stunning enough to send him reeling. That long, waterfall of blue-black hair, those dark eyes, that honey-toned skin—they all marked her as different among the patrician Ashtons. But, even more, it was her personality, the way she *was,* that made her different.

She preferred flowers to people, a bicycle to a flashy car and had an innocence that was completely at odds with the world she'd grown up in. There was something about Charlotte that was pure and untouched, a beauty of the heart that tugged at him more and more with every moment he spent with her.

Putting the basket by the tree, he spread the picnic blanket and then inclined his head. "Sit, *ma belle*. Tonight, your knight waits upon his lovely princess."

Though she was illumed only by the moonlight, he saw the flush that heated her golden skin. "You say the most wonderful things." Her eyes shimmered, large and dark.

That she trusted him enough to confess that made his rusty heart beat with newfound spirit. A twinge of guilt infiltrated the joy spreading through his blood, but he ignored it, certain that he'd done the right thing in reading her journal. How could it have been wrong, when it had brought him to this moment of pure happiness?

"What have you got in here?" Charlotte peeked into the basket, her hair falling over her breast.

"Delights to tempt and seduce you so I can have my wicked way," he drawled, teasing her when all he wanted to do was lay her down and satisfy the savage in him. He had a feeling she could make even that dangerously possessive part of him purr in satisfaction.

Looking up, she made a face at him, startling him with the playful curve of her mouth. "You shouldn't be let out to wreak havoc on the female of the species. You're positively lethal."

He was delighted that she saw him that way. "Where would you put me? In a cage?"

She shook her head, the dark silk of her hair shifting with the motion. Unable to resist, he moved closer and fingered the strands whispering over her shoulders, his eyes on her face.

"That would be a terrible waste." Though she was blushing, there was a look in her eyes that told him she was going to tease him right back. "You should be kept in a bedroom...where you can satisfy a woman's wickedest fantasies."

Six

His temperature skyrocketed. Swearing softly under his breath, he cupped her cheek and kissed the sassiness right off her lips. It tasted far too good for his peace of mind. "You mustn't say such things. I can't be expected to romance you if my body is straining with the urge to bury itself in your sweet body."

She gasped, her eyes huge and dark. "I say the boldest things around you. You're a bad influence."

He grinned. "I'd say I'm a very good influence." Reaching out with his right hand, he pulled out a pre-chilled bottle of champagne from the picnic basket. "Not the perfect temperature, but it'll do."

Charlotte held out the two champagne flutes she'd plucked. After pouring, he accepted one flute bubbling silver-gold in the darkness, his fingers running along the back of her hand. She shivered.

"I love the way you want me, kitten." His voice was low,

dark, husky, that of a lover talking to his woman. He couldn't change that, couldn't make it playful and merely flirtatious, not when the woman was Charlotte.

"You said not to talk that way," she accused, but her dark eyes held a look that told him if he did reach out and touch her intimately, she might just let him. They'd come a long way from that first kiss.

Sighing at the restraints he'd put on himself tonight, he raised his glass. "To my Charlotte. Utterly lovely. Utterly unique. And supremely luscious."

Her responding smile was unknowingly sensuous. "To Alexandre, who should be locked up for the good of the female population."

After a sip, he put aside his champagne and started pulling delicacy after delicacy from the basket. "Do you like caviar?"

She shook her head. "Awfully plebeian of me."

"I don't like it, either," he confessed. "I fail to see why people pay ridiculous sums for tiny fish eggs." Charlotte's quick giggle was unexpected. He looked up into her amused eyes. "What?"

"You drive a car that many people would consider um…an ego on wheels and you can't see the temptation to indulge in caviar?" Charlotte had no idea where her impertinence was coming from. She guessed it had something to do with the way he looked at her, like he'd just like to eat her alive, *after* savoring her with exquisite slowness. Never had she imagined that a man as powerfully masculine as Alexandre would find her that fascinating. The thought intoxicated her far more than the bubbles of champagne fizzing against her lips.

He scowled. "Don't think I didn't notice that hesitation. I can forgive the use of the word ego but anything else and I might've had to get nasty."

"Oooh, I'm scared." She wanted to kiss him. Not just because of desire, but because he'd given her this. This moment of moonlight and magic, a moment when she felt wild and beautiful and desirable, things that she'd only dreamed about being.

As if he'd read her mind, those dark chocolate eyes flared with heat. Without a word, he leaned over and kissed her like he had every right to touch her as he pleased. Her stomach went into freefall. Her toes curled. "Mmmm." Tiny pleasure sounds escaped her.

Alexandre's body tensed and his hand fisted in her thick hair. A little trace of disappointment tinged her joy at that indication of accelerating passion. No matter what he did, she'd enjoy Alexandre's touch but tonight…tonight she wanted romance. Slow kisses and gentle strokes.

"You make me forget all my vows." Then he said something steamy and dark in his native tongue. The unfamiliar word sounded mysterious and sensual, things she'd never considered herself.

Alexandre's lips descended to hers again and she felt the embers in her body ignite into flame. Ready for thunder, she was delighted to discover that he was dedicated to going slow tonight. Very slow.

His lips coaxed, tempted, teased. His tongue stroked across her lower lip, but barely ventured into her welcoming mouth. When his teeth grazed her lips, his tongue was there to soothe the sensual hurt.

"Alexandre," she murmured, reaching for him, her hand fisting in his shirt. He felt so good. So hard and hot and rawly masculine.

Below the sophisticated surface, Alexandre Dupree was very much a man. There wasn't a line of his body that was soft or relaxed. His steely control was apparent in the tautness of the muscles of his waist where her other hand landed. "You don't like this slow kissing," she said, when he let her breathe.

A smile curved his sensual lips. "On the contrary, *ma petite*. Slowly driving you crazy intrigues me." His thumb rubbed over her lower lip. Somehow, the touch tugged at something much lower in her. Much more intimate. "I could spend hours kissing you."

As if to prove that, he closed the gap between their lips once more, his hand slipping from her hair to curve around her nape, his other hand cupping her cheek. She was becoming accustomed to both gestures, but they still made her come undone. The possessiveness of the one hold, compared with the tenderness of the other, completely destroyed her capacity for rational thought. How could he do that to her without even trying?

Thinking became too hard when he ran his hand along her jaw. Charlotte sighed into the exquisitely romantic kiss and gave herself up to Alexandre Dupree's magic. Her surrender was rewarded over and over, his kisses designed to bring her the most extreme pleasure.

Alexandre used every bit of experience he had to kiss Charlotte as she deserved to be kissed. He hadn't lied to her. He could spend hours simply kissing her, drowning in the pleasure that emanated from her, feeling more male than he'd ever before felt in his life. She was such a spirited woman, quiet yet full of strength that would last a lifetime, but her bones felt so fragile under his touch, her body so very small compared to his.

He would never trust any man but himself to handle her with the care she deserved.

The fleeting thought brought a growl to the back of his throat and for a second, the kiss veered from romantic to outright marauding, but he caught himself. Romance, he forced himself to think. His kitten needed romance and moonlight tonight, not heat and raw eroticism. That would come later.

Taking a nibbling bite from the lower lip that he knew had swelled from their kisses, he parted from her. The sight of passion-drenched eyes looking up at him through a veil of blue-black lashes almost broke him.

He bit back his groan and rubbed his thumb over her moist lips. "I want to dance with you in the moonlight. I want to feel you in my arms."

"How did you know?" she whispered, those eyes completely unguarded, completely honest.

"That's a secret," he said, unwilling to spoil the moment by admitting that he'd read her journal. Rising, he held out his hand.

Without hesitation, her fingers slipped into his, slender and fine-boned, but very capable. She stood, a graceful woman with a body that had all the right curves and hollows to drive him insane. It was as if she'd been created for him alone, his most inescapable temptation, so alluring that he couldn't find the strength to break the chains slowly binding him to her.

Slipping one arm around her slender waist, he tangled his other hand with hers. Her free hand came to rest on his shoulder. "We fit perfectly." He wanted to purr in satisfaction, his mind awash with erotic images of how well they'd fit in a far more intimate sense.

"I'm not too *petite?*" She smiled at him with that lush mouth and gave him all sorts of ideas.

"*Non.* You are perfect." And she was. In his arms, she felt so right that he didn't ever want to let her go. Instead of pressing her close as his body demanded, he allowed her freedom. The position let him see her face when she glanced up at him.

"Why…?" she began and then fell silent.

He frowned, disliking the tone of her voice. "What is it?"

When she raised her head, those dark eyes were liquid midnight. "Why are you attracted to me?"

The question shook him with its directness. "You're lovely, beautiful and intelligent. Even more, you're intriguing with those secrets in your eyes, an artist with your work *and* you have a body that tempts me to thoughts that would make you blush. Is that enough?"

He saw her swallow. "I didn't expect you to say that."

"Why?"

"I suppose I thought you'd fudge—try and skim over it."

"I never tell lies when truth will serve." Guilt knocked again, but empowered by the feel of sweet Charlotte in his arms, he pushed it aside. "Come closer." It was an invitation, sweet seduction under moonlight.

She smiled and permitted him to tug her just a tiny bit nearer. It wasn't enough to turn romance to passion but it was enough to offer his taut body some relief. The distinctive scent of her skin enchanted him, part pleasure and part the sweetest pain he'd even known.

"Alexandre, this night is magic," she whispered.

And even though he'd planned it down to the last detail, Alexandre found himself agreeing with her. There had been nothing in his plans about the peace he'd found in her arms, nor about the pleasure he'd derive from such a simple joy as dancing with his lady under the moonlight.

Charlotte spent the next morning in something of a daze. She kept smiling for no reason, and once she found herself dancing around her greenhouse pretending she was still in Alexandre's arms. Laughing at her own giddy delight in the man, she forced herself to work.

Lured by the bright day, she rearranged her schedule so that she could potter around in her outdoor garden instead of working in the greenhouse. The smell of sunshine and growth brought Alexandre to mind once again.

Last night, he'd given her romance, such beautiful wonderful romance that she was still breathless from it. Despite his desire, he hadn't pushed for anything more.

It was a heady feeling to know that she could arouse such passion in a man like Alexandre, but what scared her was that they weren't just about passion. Not any longer. Not after that dance in the moonlight. And perhaps not since their very first meeting.

He was beginning to mean more and more to her. Part of her was afraid of the pain she'd have to bear when he left, but that part was overridden by her hunger to experience all she could with him. She knew herself well enough to know that this was no casual fling—no man had ever reached her as Alexandre did.

"Stop mooning and start working," she ordered herself, realizing she'd been sitting stock-still.

As she began clearing weeds, she was overcome by the feeling that she'd forgotten something. Something important. Frustratingly, no matter how hard she tried, nothing came to her.

Finally giving up, she concentrated on her wildflowers. They were a hardy breed, designed to take the vagaries of the weather from extreme heat to frosty cold. She checked on the seedlings she'd planted to make up for the older plants she'd lost the previous year.

Today was Alexandre's birthday.

Blinking at the sudden answer to the problem that had so frustrated her earlier, she sat down on the ground. Why did she know that? Was it true?

Determined to find out, she walked into the house and to her computer. In her first burst of hungry curiosity about the dark Frenchman who'd left her speechless with his sheer male presence, she'd read several articles on the acclaimed winemaker. One of them had been in a news magazine dealing with his vineyard in France, with a sidebar on him personally.

She found it after a single search-engine query. There it was in black and white. Today was Alexandre's birthday and he hadn't so much as made a reference to it last night. Then again, he was hardly the type of man who needed gifts.

But, she thought, it wasn't the gift that mattered, it was the fact that someone cared enough to give it. Smiling at having found him out, she walked to the greenhouse and began putting together a bouquet. It made her laugh to think of giving her strong, masculine wolf of a man flowers, but she wanted to give him something simple, something joyful.

From what little he'd let slip, she could tell that he was jaded by the things he'd seen in his life, but nobody could ever be jaded by the bouquet she made him. Instead of cultured roses for her wolf in sheep's clothing, she used wild roses in a vibrant yellow that would've made Scrooge himself smile.

She added several gerberas in vivid red and wildflowers in every color she could find, both from the blooms in her outdoor garden and those within her greenhouse. For a hint of mischief, she added some soft pink dahlias, velvety and lovely. Alexandre didn't have a touch of pink in him.

Her cell phone rang as she was debating how to deliver her bouquet. Grabbing it from the workbench, she said, "Charlotte speaking."

"Has anyone ever told you that you have a voice that could bring a man to his knees, *ma petite?*"

Look who's talking, she thought. "Alexandre." She grinned. "What are you doing?"

"I'm in the winery, considering the effect of the estate's

use of cultured yeast strains on the distinctiveness of its wine." He made it sound intensely interesting. The man was clearly crazy about wine.

"Sounds like fun. Are you busy for lunch?"

There was a long pause. "*Non*. Is that an invitation?"

It was the pause that made her realize it was the first invitation she'd ever extended to him. "*Oui*," she responded, wanting to make him smile.

It seemed to have become very important to her to make Alexandre smile. There was darkness in him, darkness that hurt him. While she didn't yet know the details of what haunted him, she sensed enough to know he needed smiles and laughter, teasing and play.

He chuckled. "Then I shall be there in an hour. Do you wish me to bring anything?"

"No. I'm all set. Don't tell anyone but we'll be drinking Louret wine." Spencer would've had a fit if he'd found a bottle of the "enemy" wine on his property. But, she liked Louret's signature chardonnay and if she couldn't afford to escape the estate in reality, at least she could do so when she indulged her senses.

"Your secret is safe with me."

After hanging up, Charlotte rushed back into the house and began preparing a quick lunch. Throwing some mini pizzas into the oven, she tossed together a salad, created a cheese board and found some fruit to add to it.

She frowned and decided that it wasn't enough. He was a bit larger than her, her wolf. Pursing her lips, she rummaged in the freezer and found some corn dogs. Grinning, she put them into the oven. She wondered what he'd think of those unsophisticated items of food. The final touch was to add a loaf of crusty warmed bread.

She'd just put everything on two large trays that they

could carry outside when she heard a golf cart arrive. Alexandre's voice called out a moment later. "Charlotte?"

"In here."

He prowled into her kitchen, enticing her with nothing more than his walk, his eyes, his sheer male sensuality. Before she could say a word, he kissed her. Slow and deep, it said he had all the time in the world to love her.

"*Bonjour.*" It was a husky rasp against her lips.

"Hello." She smiled, fascinated by the way he looked at her. No man had ever seen such sensuality in quiet, shy Charlotte Ashton.

"Shall I carry these out for you?" He nodded toward the trays she'd put on the kitchen counter.

"Thanks. I put the blanket down there." She pointed out the sturdy old tree behind the cottage.

Nodding, he picked up both trays. "Corn dogs?" His grin was unexpected and startlingly beautiful. "I haven't eaten one for years." Apparently happy, he headed out.

Following him with the wine that Louret had named Caroline in honor of their matriarch, she felt pleasure suffuse her. They'd had kisses and dances in the moonlight, passion and romance, but what shimmered between them this time was something just as rare—friendship.

Alexandre was in a good mood and their picnic was full of teasing and laughter. Charlotte found herself completely at ease with him, her shyness undone by his open enjoyment of her presence. She was, she thought, very close to adoring sexy Alexandre Dupree.

That awareness dawned as she was taking the remains of their lunch inside, having refused his offer of help. It didn't startle her—her feelings for this man had run shockingly deep since the moment they'd first met. If they hadn't, she could've brushed aside that first kiss instead of being so hurt by what she'd seen as Alexandre's game-playing.

Shaking off the melancholy that threatened to darken her mood at the thought of how soon he'd be leaving the estate—and her—she sneaked out to her greenhouse from the front door. After retrieving the bouquet, she walked around the house to surprise Alexandre.

He was sprawled against the tree, his shirt sleeves rolled to the elbows and his sand-colored jacket discarded carelessly to the side of the blanket. Eyes closed in relaxation, he looked very much like a large predator sunning himself after a good hunt. It wasn't until she knelt beside him that he opened his eyes.

"What's this?" He looked at the bouquet.

"Happy birthday, Alexandre." She placed the flowers in his arms and kissed him softly on the cheek.

He couldn't have looked more shocked if he'd tried. *"Ma chérie,"* he began and then seemed lost for words. When he met her gaze, she saw a vulnerability in him that tore her apart. "No one but you has ever given me flowers. I feel as if I'm holding sunshine in my arms."

She fell another step closer to adoration at the way he cradled the flowers, careful not to bruise a single bloom. "I wanted to give you a smile. You don't do it enough. Why is there such sadness in your eyes?"

"Ah, Charlotte," he murmured instead of giving her an answer. Placing the flowers aside, he held out his arms.

She went into them without hesitation, sitting herself on his lap when he tugged her up. Arms around his neck, she looked into a face softened by tenderness. "You should've told Lilah it was your birthday. She would've loved giving you a party."

He shuddered. *"Non,* thank you. I prefer not to spend my time with people who know nothing of me."

The implied statement had her heart thudding. "You're a hard man to know."

"We all have our secrets. Even you. Sometimes, I glimpse such sadness in your eyes that it's almost a physical wound. What hurts you so?"

That penetrating gaze looked at her and there was more than command in them, more than the certainty of a strong man used to getting his way. Those things, she could've resisted. But how could she resist the unhidden care, the open need to protect?

"I was three years old when I came to live here," she said quietly. "Walker was eight. We were orphans."

"Does the memory of your parents haunt you still?" His arms tightened around her.

"In a way." The pause was a chance to take a step back from this relationship. "We were told that both our parents died in a car accident, but…"

"But?"

"Even Walker doesn't believe me. He thinks I can't handle the truth—he doesn't say so because he loves me, but I know that's what he thinks."

Raising one hand, Alexandre cupped her cheek. "I don't know what it is that you believe, but you don't strike me as a woman who chases after fool's gold."

Her heart tumbled. "I have no proof…but I don't think my mother was dead when Spencer took us."

Seven

"I see." Alexandre was silent for a while. Charlotte wondered if he thought she was crazy. Sometimes, even she thought she was delusional. "Have you ever tried to find out the truth?" he asked at last.

"I've done some research on my roots." Self-consciously, she touched her raven black hair, as straight as an arrow and as glossy as polished jet. "I mean, my mother's roots."

"Then, of course, they are yours. No one can steal that from you, no matter where you were raised."

That he'd read her anxiety so easily brought a lump to her throat. "You know my mother was Lakota Sioux," she said. "I didn't remember that, but Walker did."

When Alexandre didn't interrupt, she continued, "I decided to ask Spencer about it when I was about fifteen. He said my mother came from a reservation in South Dakota." His exact words had been "some two-bit reservation in

South Dakota"—scathing, but for once, not malicious. He'd been distracted by business papers when she'd asked him the question and his answer had been instinctive.

"Were you able to trace the reservation?" There was no disbelief in Alexandre's tone.

Reassured, she decided to share what she knew. Though she'd found herself mentioning her belief to Jillian last month, she hadn't discussed it with anyone in depth. Now, held in the arms of a man she trusted and who was willing to listen, she found herself tripping over her words in an effort to convince him that she wasn't grasping at straws.

"There's a really big one called Pine Ridge—it's in South Dakota, but borders Nebraska. The people there are part of the Oglala Lakota Nation." She paused to take a jerky breath.

"I think my mother was from Pine Ridge. Spencer was born and raised in Nebraska, so it makes sense to think that my father, too, would've been in Nebraska in his youth—close enough to meet my mother."

When she looked at him, he nodded. "*Oui*, it's logical to assume this from what you know. Do you know where your parents lived after marriage?"

She shook her head. "No. Walker said that at the time of the accident we had a farm, but he couldn't remember the name of the town. All Spencer would say was that it was a dot somewhere in the middle of Nebraska—he hadn't bothered to remember the name."

She was certain that Spencer knew exactly where her parents' farm had been. Maybe he was afraid that if she learned too much, she'd expose his lies and alienate her brother from him. Walker was closer to his Uncle Spencer than their cousins were to their father, and it would destroy their relationship if she was able to prove her suspicions.

"You have a right to know where you came from."

Something in Alexandre's voice told her that he understood her emotional hunger far better than she could've imagined. "I'd like to help you in your search if you'll let me."

Charlotte's huge eyes focused on him, full of heartbreaking joy. "No one's ever believed me before," she whispered. "No one's ever listened." Wrapping her arms around his neck, she buried her face against him.

Clenching his arms tight, he held her close, suddenly aware of the vulnerability hidden behind her cool, dark gaze. "Ah, Charlotte," he murmured, rubbing her back. Distressed at her pain, he whispered soft words to her in his native language, gentling and coaxing.

After a long while, she relaxed, resting her head on his shoulder. "I thought," she began, "I might be able to trace it through her...death certificate."

"Of course." He was impressed by how far she'd come on her own. "Have you applied for a copy?"

"No," she said, shame in her tone. "I couldn't bear to be wrong. Walker is right in one sense—I don't want to admit that we lost everything. I want someone I can call Mama and have her call me daughter." Her eyes glistened with withheld pain. "I don't want her to be d-dead."

He was undone by her sorrow. Keeping Charlotte happy had become of vital importance to him. Unlike other women he knew, her emotions were never false illusions, her desperately fought tears as honest as her laughter. In mere days, he'd found himself unable to live without one and shattered by the other.

He cuddled her against him, dropping kisses on her lips, her cheeks, her stubborn little chin. When he moved his hands, her unbound hair flowed like cool water over his arm. "But," he spoke against her lips. "I think the not knowing hurts you more than the truth ever could." He believed that, though the truths he'd learned as a child had hurt him unbearably.

"I…you're right." The determination in her gaze awed him.

"I'll be with you if you need me." Though he wanted to do everything for her, find out the truth before it could hurt her, he understood her need to finish this on her own.

It was late that night when Charlotte realized Alexandre had never answered her question about what made him so sad. Caught up in her own emotional upheaval, she hadn't pressed. But, she decided, next time she would.

He was an extraordinary man, and she wanted to know all of him. It was wonderful to have someone who believed in her, but what touched her heart was that Alexandre had urged her to go after the truth. *Whatever that might be.*

Instead of dismissing her claims or giving her false hope, he'd just offered her a shoulder to lean on. It was startling to realize how much that meant. Taking a deep breath, she booted up her computer despite the late hour and logged on to the Internet.

It took only a minute to find the Web site for Nebraska's vital records office. Births, marriages…and deaths. She decided to request the death certificates of both her parents, printing out the forms to post. Though it would've been faster to order them online, she needed something tangible in her hands, proof that she was no longer cowering in fear, but moving forward.

According to the Web site, it would take a few days for the certificates to be sent to her. But what were a couple more days compared to the lifetime she'd waited to learn the truth?

It was only when her handwriting blurred in front of her that she realized she was crying. Without warning, the wrenching, never-forgotten pain of losing her parents shattered her composure, leaving her lost and broken.

Too young to have strong memories, she still remembered emotions and fragments of time. Her father's deep laughter, the sunshine on her face as she ran outside, her mother's gentle hand on her head. *And love.* Deep, warm love that had made her feel safe.

She'd never forgotten that feeling, never been able to, because after their "adoption" by Spencer, there'd been no more parental love. Walker had done his best, but she'd missed her mother so much. That feeling had only intensified as she'd grown into a young woman. And by then, she hadn't even had Walker to talk to—her beloved brother had already belonged to Spencer.

Sobbing, she felt loneliness settle over her like a heavy cloak. Only days ago, she would've borne the burden in silence, but tonight her heart rebelled. Hands trembling, she picked up the phone.

"Alexandre?" she said, when he answered sounding half-asleep.

"*Ma petite?* What is wrong?" His voice was suddenly wide-awake, colored by concern.

"I just ordered copies of my parents' death certificates." She wiped away her tears.

"Would you like me to come to your cottage?"

"I woke you up." She shoved a hand through her hair, wondering what she was doing. "I'm sorry."

"Never be sorry for contacting me if you need me." Before she could bristle, he added, "It's very nice to be needed by a woman fully capable of relying on herself."

"Charmer." Her tears had abated but she still hurt deep inside.

"I'll be there soon. Don't cry in my absence—I won't be pleased."

Half-smiling at that last order, she hung up and headed into the kitchen to make coffee. Alexandre arrived just as it finished perking. He took one look at her face and enfolded her into his strong arms, kicking the door shut behind him. His chin settled on the top of her head as she buried her face against his chest, wrapping her arms around him.

"You've been crying," he accused, as if she'd done something unforgivable.

"I do that sometimes," she said, trying to tease him.

"I don't like it when you cry. You will promise not to do it."

She smiled at the roughly uttered command. "Are you one of those men who crumbles at the first sign of tears?"

"*Non*. It is only your tears that make me so weak. So you must take pity on me."

"I made coffee," she whispered.

"I'm going to hold you first."

She made no protest. Until this man, she hadn't understood the joy of a simple embrace. Something in her melted and she knew the sensation was only going to continue the longer she stayed in Alexandre's arms.

It was a feeling she didn't want to fight. Her fears against becoming intimately involved with him faded to nothing, as she realized that time wouldn't change what she felt for him. The longer she waited, the less time she'd have with him…and she ached for every moment.

She couldn't have said how long he held her, stroking her hair and murmuring in her ear. But, when they finally separated, she felt at peace with herself. Not only had he soothed her hurt, his tenderness had given her the courage to make the decision she'd been fighting against since the first moment she'd seen him.

"You're an extraordinary man," she said, reaching up to stroke the hard line of his jaw.

Caught by the shine in her dark eyes, Alexandre shook

his head. "I'm no knight in shining armor. I wish I could be for you."

Her smile was soft. "I know a knight when I see one. Even if he thinks his armor is rusty."

He began to play with a strand of her midnight hair. "What if I told you my birth makes me a bastard, not a knight?" The deep need to know whether she'd accept the man he was overcame his long held habit of not allowing anyone too close. *Especially* not a woman.

"Alexandre Dupree, how can you be primitive enough to think that a man's birth determines who he is?" She scowled. "If you're a bastard, then I'm a half-breed."

Anger flared. He caught her chin in strong fingers. "Don't *ever* use those words to describe yourself again."

Her eyes widened but there was no fear in them, only trust so powerful, it shook him. "If you promise to do the same."

"You are a tough negotiator." He sealed their bargain with a kiss that edged on being blatantly territorial. "You're also a beautiful, unique woman—the product of a union between two people who loved each other enough to not care about difference. You should be proud."

"I wouldn't dare to be otherwise now." Her smile was luminous. "Will you tell me about your parents?"

"I think we should talk about yours today. Mine can wait." He thought she'd berate him for backing away from the personal subject, but she just shook her head at him.

"I'd like to keep my ordering of the certificates between us…until we know for sure."

"You can trust me, *chérie*. I've had a lifetime of keeping secrets."

Charlotte looked up, caught by the cynicism in that last sentence. Though Alexandre was a man of the world, sophisticated as they came, he'd never before struck her as cynical. "Are you going to tell me what you mean by that?"

His lips curved in a small smile, but there was a bruised kind of pain in those bitter-chocolate eyes. "Perhaps one day."

Instead of annoyance at his reserve, she felt a strange stab of tenderness for this man who seemed so far beyond those things. "Come here." She smiled an invitation, though she was already in his arms.

Surprise chased the pain from his beautiful eyes. "I'm at your service."

When he firmed his embrace, she raised her arms and put them around his neck. Her heart was thudding like a mad thing and she was sure her cheeks were bright red.

Before Alexandre, she'd never let men close enough to make any moves, unable to let her guard down. With this man, she'd been letting him make all the moves, but right now, she had the feeling he needed her to take the lead.

She'd called him because she'd ached to be held, but now that her need had been fulfilled, she wanted to fulfill his. This beautiful, sensual man needed tender care just as much as she did. How she knew, she couldn't say. She just did.

A delighted smile curved over his lips and spread to his eyes. "What is this, *ma petite?*" Leaning down, he met her halfway when she rose on tiptoe.

"I'd like to kiss you," she whispered, voice lost to the passion racing through her bloodstream.

"I'll never say *non* to your kiss." His arms firmed around her, tensile steel under skin gilded by the sun.

Holding herself up by her arms around his neck, she reached up and bridged the breath separating them. His lips were a brush against hers, warm and welcoming. Heart beating so hard she was afraid it would pop out of her chest, she pressed just a tiny bit harder and slanted hers at the angle she liked.

He shuddered.

Something hotly feminine in her stretched awake. Taking another chance, another step, she flicked her tongue along his lower lip. His arms locked tight, and he crushed her against him, making no effort to hide his arousal. This time, it was Charlotte who shuddered, shocked at the heat that sparked to life inside of her, as if her desire were feeding on his.

Opening her mouth, she swept her tongue along his lower lip before suckling it into her mouth. She felt a groan rumble in his chest. Then his lips pressed hard against hers, a silent order for her to stop teasing him and fully open her mouth. She almost smiled at his inability to give up control. Almost. But she was burning up inside and the only thing she wanted was to do exactly as he asked.

Her sigh as she surrendered was a final temptation, a testing of her newfound power. His reaction sent sizzling heat rocketing through her. His body seemed to go impossibly steely, so taut and hard that she felt deliciously female next to his inescapable masculinity.

As she'd come to expect, to delight in, his hand rose up her back to clench in her hair, tilting her head. In response, she pressed herself against him and wrapped her arms around him even more tightly.

Her reward was a kiss so scorching, her knees crumpled. Only Alexandre's uncompromising embrace kept her upright, the arm around her waist solid with muscle, his palm curled around the curve of her waist. With a moan, she buried her fingers in his hair and abandoned her senses to him.

Alexandre was drowning in the feel of Charlotte. It was the first time she'd ever initiated a kiss and that would've been enough for him. But she'd given him so much more, a surrender of the senses that betrayed how much she trusted him to lead this dance.

It was clear she was relying on him to stop despite their

bodies' demands for completion, because Charlotte wasn't a woman who took lovemaking lightly. And he wasn't a man who'd be satisfied with anything less than her total involvement in any intimacy. Taking a final taste of her, he ended the kiss.

Long, dark lashes lifted. Passion-clouded eyes met his. "Alexandre." It was a husky invitation. "Why did you stop?" Reaching with her body, she claimed his lips again.

He shuddered under the caress and firmed his muscles, allowing her to steal yet another kiss before pulling away, though it was the hardest thing he'd ever done. "You tempt a man past all reason."

She nuzzled his neck and planted a row of kisses along his jaw. "I love the way your jaw feels." Running her teeth along it, she nipped gently.

Alexandre felt sweat bead on his forehead. No woman had ever driven him this insane with passion. The desire to simply lay her down and teach her all sorts of ways a man could tease his woman was almost overwhelming, but he knew the importance of this moment. His shy *fleur* was awakening in his arms—her faith in him as a man had never been more apparent.

She was now kissing her way down his neck, her beautiful body sliding oh, so slowly down his, a symphony of delight that tortured at the same time. He knew he should loosen his embrace but he wanted to feel every inch of her as it rubbed over him. She didn't stop her kisses when she reached the open neck of his shirt.

The first kiss fell on the dip where his collarbones met. Alexandre felt his entire body go taut. *"Charlotte."*

Smiling against him, she kissed down to the first button of his shirt. "Can I open this button?" Her eyes were big in that exotically beautiful face.

"Non," he growled. "Definitely not. You will kill me."

"Please," she whispered, in the husky tones of a woman who has just discovered her feminine power.

It was a shock to the system in more ways than one. He'd never thought he'd be encouraging a woman's sexual strength, but faced with Charlotte's blossoming sensuality, he knew that he'd deny her nothing. "One button," he said, moving the hand still clenched in her hair to the warm curve of her nape.

Sliding her hands down from his neck, she undid the first button. Her fingers spread over the exposed triangle of skin, sending his nerve endings into overdrive. "Your hair here feels different—crisper." It was an intimate whisper from a woman to her lover.

He leaned his head closer to hers. "Do you like it?"

Her nod sent the cool water of her hair sliding over his hands. "How good is your control?" Heavily lashed eyes looked up at him, desire alive in their depths.

He had no control where she was concerned. "What is it you wish of me, *chérie?*"

Color stained her cheeks but she didn't back away. "I want to keep going."

He swallowed and tried to breathe. "All right." He knew he should stop her but he didn't have it in him. If she wanted to do this, he'd find a way to rein in the ravenous hunger awakening in his body. A hunger that wanted a long, hot taste of Charlotte.

At least twice over.

Eight

Charlotte undid another button on Alexandre's shirt and wanted to whimper. The man's body was beautiful beyond all reason. Unable to resist the temptation, she pressed her lips to the skin she'd bared, tasting him.

His groan was a rumble against her lips, his heart thunder under the fingertips she had pressed against his shirt. Glorying in her ability to make him feel such pleasure, she undid two more buttons and found herself at the waistband of his pants.

Swallowing, she pulled out the tails of his shirt and slipped the last button out of its hole. The feel of his bare skin under her hands had her gasping for breath. His abdomen was ridged with muscle that tensed under her touch and she indulged herself by running her fingers over him.

"Charlotte."

Biting her lower lip, she looked up into his face. Alexandre's eyes were closed and his jaw clenched tight, as he un-

doubtedly fought his desire to take the reins. It was the final thing she needed to tell her that she'd made the right
decision. "Alexandre?"

His lashes lifted. *"Ma petite."*

Gazing into that unapologetically masculine face, she
whispered, "Make love to me."

Alexandre felt his heart kick violently in his chest.
"Charlotte—you're emotional—don't make a decision that
will cause you hurt in the morning." He couldn't bear it if
she regretted being with him.

Her smile was soft and so bright, he felt blinded by its
beauty. "I'll never regret being loved by you."

"Are you truly sure?" he forced himself to ask, battling
the possessive marauder who just wanted to take.

"Yes."

He shuddered and held her tight. "I'm afraid I can't
protect you." Her becoming pregnant didn't scare him. For
the first time in his life, such a thing seemed a gift rather
than a worry. And that worried him. How far had Charlotte
Ashton burrowed into his heart?

She placed a gentle kiss over his heart. "Remember that
day I went to town and you got so angry because I'd walked home in the dark?"

Of course he remembered. Once again, his conscience
told him that he should confess but he couldn't bring himself to shatter her faith in him. "Yes."

"Well…I made myself buy…you know." He could feel
her blushing. "I was so embarrassed—I've never done that
before. I was sure everyone was looking at me."

He bit back his smile. "Why did you buy…you know?"
His words were gently teasing, even as relief whispered
through him. It would've been torture to walk away tonight
when in her eyes, he'd seen a welcome he'd barely allowed himself to imagine he'd ever see.

"Because," she said, "while I might not be experienced, I know myself." She finally met his gaze. "No matter what I tried to convince myself and you, I knew that sooner or later, I'd be in your arms."

It was the first time she'd admitted her inexperience, but he would've guessed, even if he hadn't read her journal. There was an innocence about her that said she'd never known a lover. "Are you happy to be here?" His heart almost stopped beating as he waited for her answer.

Her smile began in her eyes and lit her face from within. "There's no place I'd rather be."

Lover Mine,
I guess every woman dreams of the first time she'll love a man, imagines what it'll feel like, fantasizes about how he'll touch her…how he'll taste her. I'm no different.

Do you want to know what I'd like for that very first time? I suppose you expect me to tell you I want roses and moonlight, a bubble bath and scented oils. Well, I wouldn't say no to that one day.

But for that very first time, that very first touch of skin on skin, all I want is tenderness. Absolute tenderness. I want to be touched as if I am precious, as if my body fulfills your every fantasy, as if you can't bear to let me go.

Charlotte's secret longings whispered through his mind as he took her hand and followed her gentle tug toward the bedroom. His shirt was hanging open and he noted how her gaze kept straying to his chest. He couldn't fight his grin. Giving his Charlotte tenderness would require no effort at all, not when she made him feel so protective of the shine in her eyes.

"What?" she asked, when she saw his smile.

They were in her bedroom now, standing by the double bed. He reached out and ran his fingers through her unbound hair. "I like the way you want me, kitten."

Her cheeks reddened, but when she spoke, her eyes met his. "I look at you and I want to touch."

He shouldn't have been surprised by her courage in this arena, not when he'd witnessed her strength in so many other ways. "It's not something I'll ever deny you." He cupped her cheek. "Not when I can't keep my hands off you."

When she lifted her face to his, he took the hint and kissed her. It started out gentle and slowly became wilder, his hunger for her voracious. Even as he kissed her like he'd dreamed of doing, his hands roved over her body and slipped under the bottom of her thin sweater. The feel of her warm skin was pure pleasure.

She whimpered into his mouth as his hands stroked the skin of her waist and back, but made no move to retreat. He paused long enough to ask, *"Oui?"*

Eyes big, she nodded. And then she raised her arms so he could pull the sweater off. He took his time. He'd never seen skin as beautiful as hers, tawny gold and heated with life. His eyes dropped to her stomach. She sucked in a breath.

He wanted to caress that skin but before he could, he had to bare her. He had to give the hunger in him something to feast on. With one tug, he pulled the sweater off and threw it to the floor. She stood before him dressed in jeans and a lacy white bra.

For a moment, he lost any skill he might've had, any finesse. All he wanted to do was indulge his senses in her. Shuddering, he wrapped one arm around her waist, tugged her to him and buried his face in her neck. The heady scent of her shot through his system like a drug.

"Alexandre?" Her fingers whispered through his hair as she held him to her.

Sliding his free hand up her side, he nibbled at the skin pressed so temptingly against his mouth. A shiver shook her body and in his hair, her hand clenched. It was that reaction which gave him back his control.

Tonight was about Charlotte. He could indulge himself later, once he'd plied her with pleasure. He'd make this night perfect for her. She deserved nothing less.

He murmured a question to her about the protection. Her response was breathed against his cheek. "In the bedside drawer."

Then he stopped thinking about anything aside from making Charlotte feel adored, cherished, beautiful. Moving his lips from her neck, he kissed his way along her jaw and captured her mouth once more. She kissed him back with passion and heat, the sensuality in her nature rising to the surface.

His arousal pushed at the softness of her belly as she arched against him and he had to clench his fists tight to restrain the urge to plunder. Taking a shuddering breath, he relaxed one hand and ran the fingers along her back at the point where bare skin ended and her waistband began.

She pressed closer, a silent invitation for him to take what he wanted. What he wanted most of all was to have his Charlotte naked so he could worship her luscious body from head to toe. Suckling her lower lip into his mouth, he flicked open the button on her jeans.

Their mouths parted as she made a little noise and pulled away. He halted, but realized in seconds that she wasn't saying no. She just wanted to watch. He should've guessed that a woman so intrinsically sensual would want to savor every moment.

Her eyes lowered to where his hand slowly slid down

her zipper. He'd intended to pull her jeans off but with her sultry gaze locked on his hand, he decided to tease her a little—show her that between them, this act would always include tenderness, affection and joy.

At that moment, it didn't occur to Alexandre why it was so very important to him that Charlotte was in no way hurt by this intimate dance, physically or emotionally. Heart thundering, he slipped his hand through her parted zipper and cupped her through her panties.

Jerking, she clutched at his upper arms. He tightened the hand he had around her waist and moved the hand between her legs just enough to tantalize. Gasping for breath, she looked up at him and made a silent request for more.

"What do I get if I give you more?" he asked aloud, teasing, tempting, playing.

Eyes going wide, she licked her lower lip…and then moved against him.

Once.

Twice.

"I think, *ma petite,*" he said, his voice gone rough, "you're going to drive me crazy." He withdrew his hand before the feeling of her damp and hot against him succeeded in destroying his teeth-gritting control.

She pouted a little. "Alexandre."

He pushed her jeans off her hips and to the floor. "Lift your foot for me, kitten." When she complied, putting her hands on his shoulders for balance, he completed the removal of the denim barrier.

Then he glanced up. A dark-eyed siren looked down at him, all sun-kissed skin and midnight hair. Dressed in a white lace bra and matching panties, she looked sexier than a woman had any right to look.

At his continued silence, her hands tugged at his shoulders. As he rose, he ran his fingers up the backs of her legs, luxuriating his senses in the feel of her. She shivered under his touch, especially when he passed over the curve of her bottom.

He kissed her again, tempted by the lushness of her lips, slightly swollen from his earlier caresses. Her arms slipped under his shirt and clutched at his waist, her grip firm and just a tad possessive. He liked the way she was beginning to touch him, liked the fact that she considered him hers.

Accommodating the request she communicated to him by tugging at the material of his shirt, he shrugged it off. She sighed into the kiss and rubbed herself against his skin. He thought he'd lose his mind at the feel of her breasts teasing him through satin and lace.

Aware that his restraint was dangerously close to shattering, he guided her to the bed. "Will you lie down for me?"

Clearly reluctant to stop touching him, she climbed onto the sheets. The beautiful view of her heart-shaped bottom had his erection pounding. Thankfully, she lay down on her back seconds later, giving him a moment's relief. Until she raised a hand and reached for him.

With a rumbled groan, he kicked off his shoes and shucked his pants. Unwilling to shock her with the blatant evidence of just how much he wanted her, he kept on his briefs as he followed her onto the bed.

Then, taking a deep breath, he ran his hand down her sweetly curved body. His throat locked as the marauder in him roared with need. She was perfection. Absolute perfection. He had no need to pretend she fulfilled his every fantasy—it was true. He'd never been with a woman who was so much everything he desired.

Tenderness, he thought, recalling the words he'd read in her journal. Of course he'd give her tenderness this first night—that was not something she should've been worried about receiving from her first lover. *From him.*

"Why are you so quiet?" Charlotte's big eyes were looking into his, a touch of worry in them.

He wanted to erase even that smidgen of discomfort. "I'm simply indulging myself with the sight and feel of you," he said honestly. "You're so lovely, I could gaze at you for hours, though I admit I'd want to touch far too much to resist." So saying, he ran his hand to the curve of her hip and spread his fingers.

She was blushing, the worry gone. "I should've guessed you'd say something outrageous." Her lips tilted up.

Learning down, he nibbled on her for a while, teasing her with almost kisses. He didn't rush despite the tightness in his groin. Tonight, the woman in his arms needed slow seduction, not dark heat.

"You taste better every time I kiss you," he murmured. "I'm addicted to you, *chérie*."

She ran her hands up his chest to his shoulders. "Your voice—you could seduce me over the phone."

He grinned, delighted. "I shall do my best whenever you're away from me." Leaning closer, he urged her to wrap her arms around his neck as he pressed his chest lightly against her breasts.

She shivered. "You feel so good."

"Why do you sound surprised?" He chuckled and kissed the side of her neck, slipping his hand under her body to undo the clasp of her bra.

Her hands slid from his neck into his hair, playing with the sensitive skin of his nape. This time, *he* shivered. He felt her smile against him as he continued to taste the skin above her pulse.

"I never thought it would be this wonderful to just have a man's weight on me."

He lifted his head to glare at her. "*My* weight, not any other man's."

Eyes locked with his, she slid the bra down her arms and threw it off the bed. "I didn't know you existed before," she said, a teasing light in her eyes.

It was an effort to not immediately caress her lush breasts, pressed so temptingly against him. "So who did you imagine would hold you so?"

Her smile turned into something far more sultry. "I think I always dreamed of you without knowing it."

Mollified, he kissed her until she gasped for breath and then resumed his languid stroking of her body, from breast to thigh, indulging himself even as he stoked her desire to fever pitch. Her skin was so damn beautiful, he wanted to kiss every inch of it. Did he have the patience tonight? Could he survive the passionate torture?

Shuddering, he kissed her cheekbones, then the line of her jaw, before moving to her shoulders and her collarbones. When she clenched her fingers in his hair and sighed, he knew he'd find the patience he needed to give her this tenderness.

And then he began caressing every sweet inch of her skin that he hadn't yet savored. Erotic ecstasy laced his blood at the taste on the curve of her breasts, and he had to take her into his mouth. She arched as he tugged at a nipple, her desire open and sensually beautiful. When he finally had his fill—for the moment—her breasts were sheened by the touch of his lips, her chest heaving with her attempts to suck in air.

As he moved his hands over her, intent on this slow loving, his fingers touched the lace of her panties. Frustrated at being unable to touch her without hindrance, he tugged them off and threw them aside. Then he continued on his quest to taste every secret hollow and curve.

It was an intoxication of the senses, an initiation into the arts of pleasure by a master. Charlotte felt her body arch as Alexander's long-fingered hand lingered over the planes of her stomach, the strength of him compelling.

He kissed the edge of her mouth. "You're tense, *ma petite*. Is this not to your liking?"

How could he ask that question when she was burning from the inside out? Swallowing, she turned to face him, as always, stunned by the sheer beauty of him. "I've never felt this much."

His hand slid down her hip to rest on the sensitive skin of her upper thigh, his fingers so close to the heated place between her legs that she felt like begging him to take the next step. "I'm rushing you, Charlotte." The way he said her name was a temptation, an invitation by a fallen angel to join him in sin.

"If you go any slower, I'll melt at your feet."

His smile was wicked. "Ah, but it's not your feet that I want to melt, kitten." That seducing hand curved, the fingers brushing over the delicate skin of her inner thigh. A moan escaped her.

"You're so very sensitive." His husky murmur was a purr against her ear. "The idea of spiriting you away to my chalet, for my eyes only, is looking more and more attractive."

Turning her head, she met that dark gaze. "I'm no trophy," she found herself saying, barely aware why it was so important to her that he understood that.

Intensity flared in his expression. "*Oui*—you're far more prized than a mere trophy."

She ran her fingers across his lips and he kissed the tips before bending his head and capturing her mouth again. Against her body, the hard heat of him pulsed, making her want to rub against him as he kissed her with passion and heat…and heartbreaking tenderness.

The last vestiges of shyness and uncertainty disintegrated under Alexandre's exquisite gentleness. Wrapping her arms around his neck, she kissed him back with every ounce of passion in her. She'd been saving it for a lifetime. For her dream lover—her Alexandre.

He shuddered in her arms and she felt him reach blindly into the drawer beside the bed. Frustration in his groan, he broke the kiss only long enough to find what he needed and then his lips were taking her again, hot and sensuous and unashamedly possessive.

No matter what happened afterward, tonight she belonged to Alexandre Dupree. And he belonged to her.

He whispered something French in her ear, as if he'd forgotten she couldn't speak it and shifted off her. Moments later, he returned to the kiss, pressing the length of his body against hers. She jerked at the shock of sensual heat that sizzled between them as their naked bodies came in full contact.

There was nothing separating them now, nothing but their own searching hands and hungry mouths. When his hand stroked the inner skin of her thigh, she trembled and spread her legs for him.

Gently, so gently, he guided one over his back. She followed with the other, enclosing him in a prison of desire. He trailed a rain of kisses from her mouth down her neck to her breasts, as his hand slipped between their bodies to touch her with stark intimacy.

She gasped. But there was no self-consciousness in her, only pleasure. How could it be anything else when the man parting her slick folds looked at her as if her hunger for him was purest temptation?

As she grabbed at his shoulders, he began to make love to her with his fingers, rubbing and fondling, teasing and caressing. When she moaned, he lavished attention on her breasts, too, doubling the firestorm of erotic heat. She was aware of his fingers asking for entrance into her body and she responded by pushing toward him, drunk on the scent of desire, more than ready to have him inside her.

Those elegant fingers were very strong…and very careful. He caressed her deep inside, seeming to relish her every broken moan, occasionally leaving her sensitized breasts to sip at her mouth.

Unable to speak, she kissed and touched in turn, feeding her sensual need by tracing and holding onto the muscled planes of his back. He nipped at her neck when her fingers trailed over his buttocks, shocking a tiny quiver deep inside her body, where his fingers continued to do their magic. She almost panicked at the aching depth of sensation.

A hoarse male chuckle sounded in her ear as his lips trailed along the shell. "Don't fight it, kitten. I'll hold you safe. I give you my promise." And then he kissed her again and his tongue did something to her mouth that shattered her.

She stopped breathing as pleasure splintered her thoughts into a million pieces, as the most intimate of her muscles clenched around him again and again. Her body arched under his as the darkness of pleasure engulfed her but he kept his promise—he held her safe.

Sucking in a breath after she could think again, she said, "I wanted you with me."

Her declaration made all that beautiful male muscle turn to steel around her. "I'll be with you this time." Removing his fingers from her pleasure-weakened body, he rose over her.

When he pushed for entrance into her, her sensitive flesh shuddered with aftershocks. Wrapping her arms and legs around him, she welcomed him. And when he tore through the finest of barriers inside her, she barely noticed it, the pain lost under the delight.

This time, his kiss was carnal but his body remained

still, letting her get used to the feel of him inside her, stretching her so completely that she ached. But the ache promised such absolute ecstasy that she whimpered for him to give her more.

Kissing the sound off her lips, he pushed again and lodged fully in her. Her breath fractured on a groan as he began to move and their lips finally parted. Inside her, he was a living brand, hot and powerful. Slow and deep, his loving stoked the embers of her desire and she felt another firestorm approaching. Looking into his eyes, she saw the storm mirrored in eyes gone black with passion restrained.

For *her.*

She wanted to tell him that it was okay, that he could let go now, but before she could find the words, stars began to explode in front of her eyes, the weight of his body and his scent overwhelming her senses. But, as if he'd heard her silent permission, his body arched and she knew he'd thrown the reins of control aside.

This time, he came with her.

Nine

Charlotte felt completely boneless. She lay on top of Alexandre, her face buried in his neck, breathing in his maleness and feeling the woman in her sigh. This was her mate and she reveled in him.

A big hand stroked down her back and came to rest on her bottom, possessive and certain of his right to touch her so intimately. "Are you awake?"

Velvet and danger, she thought, that's what his voice sounded like. Velvet to sensuously wrap around her and danger to tempt. "A little." Smiling against his skin, she made a valiant effort and raised her head. "I'm not sure I'm capable of rational thought though."

His eyes glinted with amusement. "You flatter me."

She laughed. "Credit where credit's due." An unexpected thought intruded on her happiness, stealing away a little of the sunshine.

"What is it? Are you hurting?" Concern, sharp and intent, layered his question. The hand that had been stroking her with languid ease was suddenly a band of steel locking her to him.

"No. I'm fine." Leaning down, she pressed a kiss to his jaw. "I'm being silly...will you be offended if I ask you something very personal?"

His arm relaxed. "We've just shared something very personal, *ma chérie*. We've claimed certain rights over each other—so ask."

"You're very good at this," she whispered. "I suppose I'm jealous of the women who came before me."

She expected him to say something sophisticated and French, something charming and teasing. Despite what he'd said about claiming, he was a man used to lovers, not at all like her, for whom a sharing of the body could only come with a sharing of the heart.

Long fingers stroked down her face. "I always respected the women I was intimate with, so I won't say that they meant nothing. But what we shared this night—it has little to do with experience and skill and everything to do with us. Nothing has ever been this powerful, this beautiful."

She adored him all the more for his honesty. This man would never treat her as lesser because she was a woman. Even more, by accepting that what they'd shared was special, he'd given her a glimpse into his heart. She could do no less.

"I've never been with another man," she said, looking down into his face, "but I know I'll never regret this. You're the only lover I could imagine spending this first night with."

His jaw tightened. "Perhaps you shouldn't imply having other lovers around me, Charlotte."

Though the words were light, the tone was anything but. Not having expected possessiveness from her sophisticated Frenchman, she couldn't help but feel joy at this sign of deeper feeling on his part.

Smiling, she folded her arms flat across his muscular chest and put her chin on her hands. "Have you ever been in love?" she asked, encouraged by his openness.

His cheeks creased with male amusement and that stroking hand began to wander over her body again. "When I was a pup of twenty, I believed myself madly in love."

"And?"

"Celeste was rather lovely, flashing blue eyes, long blond hair. I thought she was the epitome of grace."

Jealousy sunk her fangs into Charlotte once again. "I see." She fingered her own ebony mane.

Alexandre's chuckle rubbed along her skin. "You should be careful. Otherwise, I might begin to believe that you care."

"You already know I care." She made a face at him. "Why didn't you marry Celeste?"

"I decided it would be imprudent to marry a woman who was gracing all of my friends' beds."

Charlotte blinked. "What?"

"She didn't want to—how do you say—put all her eggs in one basket. The only thing she cared about was hooking a rich man. One of my former friends wasn't as fortunate as me. He's now her husband."

"I'm sorry."

"I'm not. At the time, of course I was devastated. It passed. And I was able to see the fate I'd escaped. Raoul never knows where his wife is—I would've never tolerated such a marriage."

She chewed over what he'd revealed. "Is that why you keep your attachments so short and simple? Because you don't trust women with commitment?"

His eyes darkened. "What do you know of my attachments?"

"Only what I've read in the magazine articles I could

find on the Internet," she admitted. "You don't seem to have long relationships."

"I see that you've taken my advice and are questioning me after we've made love."

It took her a moment to recall his teasing words. "I'm sorry, I didn't mean to. I wasn't trying to be manipulative." She was genuinely afraid that he'd suspect her of such base motives.

He tugged at a strand of her hair. "How can I believe such a thing when your big brown eyes are so honest?" Sighing, he shifted their positions so that they were lying side by side, face-to-face.

She put her hands on his chest and cuddled closer. "I'm glad you know that. I wouldn't want anything to spoil this night."

He smiled and wrapped his arms around her. "That would be impossible. There is magic in the air tonight."

Seduced by the warmth in his eyes, she playfully scraped her teeth along his shoulder. He jerked in surprise and then narrowed his eyes at her. "So, kitten, you want to play?"

Delighted by the passionate look in his eyes, the husky timbre of his voice, she tugged one of his hands to her mouth and delicately nibbled on his fingers. He let her have her way for perhaps a minute before a rumble sounded deep in his chest and he switched positions again, placing her atop his body.

"Come, let us play." Then he grinned and ran the nails of his hands very gently up the outside of her thighs.

Shivering, she sat up on his body, a little shy but not enough to forego the experience being held out to her by her sexy lover. "Yes," she whispered. "Let's."

An hour later, Charlotte was lying on her back, smiling dreamily and getting dozy, when Alexandre spoke. "Celeste didn't really change the core of the man I am. I'd learned my lessons long before then."

The realization that he was answering her earlier question had her drowsiness replaced by alert concentration. "Who taught you?" she dared to ask, wonder blooming in her. Alexandre wasn't a man who trusted lightly.

His answer was oblique. "My *maman* is very French, very sophisticated."

That sensually accented voice slid over her body like a physical caress. She couldn't help the tiniest of shivers.

"You're cold." Sitting up, he pulled a spread over them. The sight of his gloriously muscled back had her gulping. She could barely believe she now had the right to touch this magnificent male.

He lay down beside her, slipping his arm under her head and pulling her close. Wanting to see his face, she shimmied up until her chin was resting on his sculpted chest once again. That gorgeous face looked down at her with a distinctly proprietary glint in his eyes.

"What do you mean, sophisticated? Is she one of those elegant Parisian women they always show on the fashion shows?"

He smiled, his cheeks creasing. "*Oui,* she is most certainly elegant, *Maman.* But, I think you'd like her. She is a strong woman."

"What about your father?"

"My *papa* is a very rich man, well-respected and highly sought after in society. His wife is a British blue blood."

She didn't know how to understand what he was telling her. "Your mother was his mistress?"

"Not was, *is.* She has been with him for the longest time. As I said, *Maman* is very sophisticated and so is he. So am I."

Despite the silky charm, the world-weary tone, she

heard the pain. "Did you always know?" She wanted to hold him, soothe his hurts, but knew that a man as strong as Alexander Dupree would never accept anything that blatant.

"*Oui, ma petite.* As a child, I knew *Papa* had to leave us to go to another family. I also knew never to call him *Papa* if we should meet in public." He slid his hand down her body and she moved to accommodate him, aware that the touch was no longer sexual.

"Of course his wife knows of me and so do his other children. I'm an open secret—we French are so very mature about such things." His lips curved. "I believe his wife has a younger lover."

"Why did they ever marry?" She blurted out, unable to understand. Spencer was a bastard of a man, but at least his marriages and affairs had had some reason, be it wealth or lust.

"Money, sweet Charlotte. Money. It was understood that their families must merge to create an empire." His hand tangled in her hair.

"Does your mother…?" She stopped, aware that she might be going too far.

"I'm not offended, *chérie.* Your questions have honesty—that has never caused any harm. *Maman* was born poor. I can't fault her for choosing the life of a pampered mistress over that of working menial jobs until both her beauty and spirit died.

"We've never spoken of it, but I believe she enjoys her life. Not only does she have a lover who dotes on her, a son who respects and loves her, she has wealth and more importantly, she has freedom."

"I just—I'm afraid I have trouble understanding such lives."

"Ah, I've shocked you. I forget that you see the world through a lens I have lost."

She frowned. "Will you be as sophisticated in your marriage?" Why was she asking this when she knew that what they had would end as soon as Alexander's time at the vineyard was over? A woman like her couldn't capture a man like him, whatever feelings they'd both admitted to. Yes, she was special to Alexandre, but not special enough to hold him. How could she be, when none of those other far more experienced beauties, had ever succeeded?

Alexander rolled them both until he was braced over her, lips curved in a half smile. She couldn't read the look in those enigmatic eyes. His hand slid over her torso to enclose one breast.

"I'd never tolerate such a marriage. If my wife touched another man, I'm afraid I'd be most unsophisticated." A warning flickered in his eyes. "Some might say I'd react primitively."

She licked her lips at the wild air about him, extremely sure that a wife who strayed on Alexander Dupree would learn the very meaning of danger. "What about you?"

"Hmmm?"

"Does the same rule apply to you or are you free to keep a mistress?"

His thumb plucked at her nipple. "To ensure that his wife doesn't stray, a man must spend much time ensuring her pleasure. I intend to be very diligent in my husbandly duties. It would leave no time for distractions." Leaning down, he placed a wet kiss on her neck, nibbling his way up to her lips.

The hand on her breast continued to play with the exquisitely sensitive bud of her nipple. "*Maman* says I have a primitive nature—possessive and loyal. She doesn't know where I get it from, when neither of my parents know the meaning of possession."

Charlotte understood it absolutely. Right now, it was

blazing in his eyes. It would be a challenge being married to this man, for he'd demand complete surrender at times and complete loyalty always. But, she thought, he'd give so fully to his woman that those moments of submission would be gifts from his wife to him, a pleasure for both, a meeting of equals.

She ached to have him belong to her, this man who touched her with tender heat and looked at her with passion in his gaze. Yet, behind the passion was pain. Alexandre had been hurting his whole life and his charming facade couldn't hide that from her. Not when she looked at him with eyes full of a blossoming love.

Tonight, she'd hold him in her arms. Tomorrow, she'd think about how to go about healing his hurts until he began to believe in love and forever and commitment.

Alone in her greenhouse the following day, Charlotte mulled over what she'd learned about the man she was falling in love with, though she'd tried so very hard to keep her heart from jumping headfirst into pain.

He hadn't ever had a father who was proud to call him son. Instead, he'd been schooled from a young age to never expect the man who'd fathered him to acknowledge him in public. In effect, he'd been taught that he was shameful.

What had that done to a man of Alexandre's pride and heart? What had it done to the boy he'd been? Charlotte wanted to strangle his parents. Alexandre was loyal to his mother and she could understand why, but there was cynicism in his eyes when he spoke of her. He might be loyal to her, but he wasn't blind to her flaws.

Not only had his childhood been a mockery, the only other woman he'd trusted, Celeste, had betrayed him. Alexandre had never indicated that he didn't trust a woman's loyalty, but she could read between the lines. From what he'd seen of women, he didn't think that they could remain true to a man.

He'd said that his mother had been with his father for the longest time. So who else had she been with? Who else had a young and vulnerable Alexandre seen her with? Then there was his father's wife, with her younger lover.

Putting down the secateurs she'd been using to trim away dead leaves, she moved to the workbench. As she sorted through the heavily scented blooms she'd placed there, she knew she had to make Alexandre see that things could be different. But how could she, a woman who barely knew herself, reach the heart of this magnificent man she found herself entangled with?

"*Ma petite,* you have a most serious expression on your lovely face." Alexandre's body pressed against her back, his arms slipping around her waist. A kiss on the side of her neck sent goose bumps whispering along her arms.

"What are you doing here? I thought you were with Trace and James?" Her heartbeat accelerated at his nearness—as always, she was ultimately susceptible to him.

"We've finished our discussion and I've come to take you to lunch."

Disappointment weighed down her floating sense of euphoria. "I can't. I have to finish this." She gestured at the blood-red roses before them. "It's a special order from Mrs. Blackhill for her daughter's sixteenth birthday."

Personally, Charlotte had thought the requested flower arrangements too heavy and sophisticated for a sixteen-year-old's party, but after encountering Trina Blackhill, she'd realized that there was a big difference between the sixteen-year-old girl she'd been and the heavily made-up teenager she'd met.

"Can you not take a break with me for an hour?" His

fingers tangled with hers. "I find myself missing your company, kitten."

She bit her lip, undone by the husky reference to their night of loving. "I can squeeze out forty minutes."

"Then it's just as well that I brought a picnic basket, is it not?"

"Alexandre!" She turned in his arms, delighted. "How do you know me so well?"

Something that was almost guilt danced in his eyes. "Because I adore you."

Alexandre looked down into that lovely face and wanted to tell her about reading her journal, his nature protesting against continuing the lie of omission. But he had a feeling that if he admitted what he'd done, she'd retreat from him faster than he could think. Charlotte was an intensely private woman and he'd taken that privacy away from her.

And yet, he didn't regret it, not for a moment, not for an instant. If he hadn't found her journal, she'd still be backing away from him, refusing to let him inside that shell she'd grown to protect herself.

"Come, I've brought a wonderful wine for you to taste." He held out his hand.

"One of ours?" She let him lead her from the greenhouse to the golf cart he'd parked outside.

"Of course not. This is the best wine in the world." He gave her a smug smile as he picked up the basket from the passenger seat. "It's one of mine."

Her laugh was infectious. "Does Trace know you say that?"

"Why do you think he asked for my help in raising the profile of this winery among connoisseurs? You're commercially successful, especially with your Brute Cuvee Sparkling, but in this region, Louret is far ahead of you in terms of wines of distinctiveness."

Charlotte's lips twisted. "I hope they keep beating Spencer."

Alexandre's felt his brows rise. "You're not behind the Ashton Estate label?"

"I have nothing against it. I just like it that Louret is a big thorn in Spencer's side. After what he did to..." She paused. "You don't want to hear all this."

He led her to a sunny spot by her cottage, next to the tree where they'd previously picnicked. After spreading a picnic blanket on the ground, he set the basket on it and tugged her down to sit beside him. "Of course I do. Anything that concerns you is of great interest to me."

She let him hold her. "Oh, it's nothing new. Thanks to the recent scandal, most people know that Spencer married Caroline Lattimer and basically stole this place from her." She blew out a breath between her teeth. "I don't want to talk about him. He always makes me lose my appetite."

Alexandre chuckled. "Then we shall talk about other things."

They had a wonderful time. Charlotte was overjoyed by the pure happiness on Alexandre's face as he spoke to her without any hint of reserve. "You're not worrying over things?" he asked.

Trust him to remember the papers she'd posted to Nebraska today. "No. I've done what I can—I have to keep living life no matter what happens."

With pride in his eyes, he nodded.

All too soon, it was time to say goodbye. "I'll ride up when someone arrives to ferry over the flowers for the birthday party. Maybe you can sneak me a kiss?"

"When do you think you'll come up? I would certainly not want to miss a chance to kiss you."

"Aim for around six-thirty."

* * *

Just before six-thirty that evening, Alexandre drove a golf cart up to the estate house, intending to return to the winery after he'd claimed his kiss. There was something he wanted to finish looking at. His smile of anticipation died as he glimpsed Charlotte standing in the drive, talking to a young man.

Behind the boy, he could see a flashy red car. From the gift-wrapped package in his hand, he surmised that the boy was a party guest who'd arrived early. He caught the last of their conversation as he walked up from their blind side.

"Are you sure?" the boy asked, a smile on his face. "I could show you a good time."

"I'm afraid I'm involved with someone." Charlotte's tone was firm. "Thank you for the invitation."

"Well, when you get sick of the other guy, give me a call." He pressed a card into her hand.

Jealousy was not an emotion Alexandre was familiar with, but as he reached Charlotte and turned her in his arms, it gripped him by the throat. "She won't be needing that." Taking the card from Charlotte's hand, he slid it into the pocket of the boy's jacket. "I believe you have somewhere to be."

Without another word, the boy turned and left. Alexandre had a feeling that it had something to do with the look in his eyes.

Charlotte's soft chuckle had him glancing down. "Well, you're handy to have around. Thanks for the help. He was a tad persistent."

"An admirer, *chérie?*"

She rolled her eyes. "Just another playboy guest."

"You get such invitations often?" He was feeling very, very edgy but kept his tone amused through sheer effort of will. If he let her see the effect a little harmless flirting had

had on him, she might begin to guess at the depth of his feelings for her. And he wasn't even ready to admit those to himself.

She shrugged. "They don't matter. Now, kiss me."

His kiss was just this side of ravenous, his hunger held on the tightest of leashes. He wanted to possess, to brand, but he let her go with a caress that left her breathing deeply, eyes shiny with desire.

"Will you come to me tonight?" Her voice was soft.

He shouldn't go to her in his current mood. "I'll come."

Ten

Alexandre had seduced and coaxed and given Charlotte the kind of loving she'd fantasized about. But tonight, only a day after their first night together, he felt anything but gentle, anything but tender. He felt raw and hungry and his arousal was almost painful.

If he went to her as he'd promised, he knew that he'd scare her. She was a sensual woman, the most wonderfully responsive lover he'd ever had, but she wasn't ready for the wildness driving him. Neither was he. He'd never felt this raging need to brand a woman as his, to drive into her so deeply that he was embedded in her psyche, buried in the molten core of her.

He knew his jealous possessiveness was without foundation—Charlotte wasn't the kind of woman who'd encourage another man while involved with him. But the fact was, that guest had been hitting on *his* woman. Coldly discouraging the youth's advances hadn't been enough to calm the marauder he was at heart, turbulent and domineering.

He hungered to go to her. He wanted to strip her naked and rub his beard-roughened jaw across her sensitive skin. Not hard. Never painfully. Just enough to mark her a little, just enough to calm himself. Except he knew that even that wouldn't be enough.

This time, he needed absolute surrender.

Compliance.

Obedience to his every sensual desire.

Sometimes, I wonder what it would be like to give you such complete trust that I'd do anything you asked, without question…without hesitation.

Yes, she'd dreamed of playing an intimate game of control and submission, but if he went to her, it wouldn't be about fulfilling her fantasy. Tonight, he wanted to take for himself, to indulge his needs and not hers. He would of course ensure she found pleasure, that wasn't even a question, but it would be on *his* terms.

Pacing the guestroom, Alexandre gritted his teeth and accepted that he couldn't go to her in this state. Not for anything did he want to scare her. But neither could he remain in this room without going insane. A few seconds later, he was by the doors that led out to the second floor terrace. Before heading down the steps that led from the terrace to the ground, he set the latch to ensure the doors would lock behind him.

And then he started walking, his aim to exercise off the pounding, almost hurtful need in his belly. He didn't pay any attention to where he was heading, focusing only on the burn of muscle as his legs strode over the ground.

Some time later, he looked up and halted in shock. Charlotte's cottage lay barely a dozen feet away. Even after deciding not to inflict himself on her, he'd come to her, driven by impulses beyond his control.

He stared at the rectangle of light in the bedroom window. So, his lover was still awake. Waiting for him? Immediately, any good the long walk might've done was gone. He was rock hard, so aroused that he thought he might die if he didn't have her. Clenching his fists in the pockets of his dark slacks, he turned, intent on going back.

"Alexandre? Is that you?"

Startled, he spun around. She was standing in the doorway of the cottage, barely covered by a white shirt. Immediately, he scowled. "Why are you standing there dressed like that when you didn't know who it was?" He couldn't control the harsh rebuke in his tone. Charlotte aroused his most protective instincts and they had nothing of sophistication about them.

"I only opened the door fully when I realized it was you. Why are you prowling out there?" She took a step out the door.

"Stop right there."

"Why?" Hurt echoed in her voice.

"Don't sound like that—it kills me." He blew out a harsh breath. "I'm on edge tonight. I can't be sure what I'll do to you if you're silly enough to let me get my hands on you."

She started moving again. "That sounds very intriguing. What do you think you might do to me?"

He *growled* at her, losing his civilized veneer as she came dangerously close, close enough that he could tumble her to the ground and take her right now. The stark eroticism of the image ripped his already tenuous control to shreds.

"You must go back inside." He forced the words out. "Right now, I can't be the lover you need—I want you in a way that would shock you to your toes. I want you hot and wet and writhing under me. Definitely *under* me," he murmured, his proprietary instincts taking over as he glimpsed the sensual curiosity in her eyes.

"I want to drive into you so completely that you forget I'm not a part of your body. I want to touch your breasts and legs and anything else I please, any way I like, for so long as I choose. I want your reaction, your cries, your hunger, but I don't want you to be an equal party. I want you to surrender to me. Without compromise."

Charlotte swallowed at the description of just what her not-so-sophisticated Alexandre wanted from her. He looked like a wild wolf, undisciplined and ravenous. *For her.* Only she would do, she realized slowly, the femaleness in her exulting at having enticed such an intriguing male.

She refused to turn away from him tonight, not when he'd given her such tenderness the night before. The commitment implied by his starkly possessive words stunned her. This went beyond pleasure, beyond desire. Was she ready to accept the claim he wanted to make?

Mouth dry, she raised her fingers to the hem of her shirt and without giving herself time to think about it, tugged it over her head, leaving herself naked. "I'm all yours," she whispered, dropping the shirt to the ground.

He didn't ask for any more permission. Instead of ravaging her, he moved around her, stalking, prowling, as if he were inspecting every inch of her. The look in those sinful eyes was distinctly proprietary. It made her feel treasured, desired, wanted. There was no room for embarrassment or shame—his open need for her gave her the confidence she needed. As a woman. As a lover.

The throbbing between her legs increased, beating in time to the rapid thudding of her heart. She needed to touch him, but he'd asked for complete surrender and she'd acquiesced. So she remained silent and let her wild wolf move to her back.

His hands settled on her hips. She jumped.

"I'm going to take you out here, with the darkness and

the stars for company." It was a husky description. Moving her hair aside, he kissed her neck, nipping at her. "I so enjoy the way you taste, kitten."

After his words of raw hunger, she expected him to take her quickly. There was no fear in her. She trusted Alexandre to care for her, even in his passion. And she was ready for him. He brought the sensual, pleasure-seeking woman in her to the surface, turned fantasy to reality.

Strong hands roamed down her body. One slipped between her legs, shocking a gasp out of her. Seconds later, it slid down her thigh, urging her to part her legs. Feeling wild and untamed and uninhibited, she did as he asked, shifting her stance so that she was shamelessly open.

His fingers feathered through her curls and then they were gone. She felt his body heat and nothing more. A second later, his hands were on her hips and his shoulders were wedging her thighs apart and his mouth was on her like a brand. Her legs threatened to crumple as sensations bombarded her, hot and vicious and pleasurable enough to make her drunk. One big hand slid up to flatten against her belly and he began to knead her taut flesh, even as his tongue did things to her that had her shaking in reaction. Clutching at the hand on her abdomen, she widened her stance even more, unable to resist his silent request.

The hand on her hip clenched, the thumb rubbing across her sensitized skin. "*Tu es très belle.* You are so beautiful." His words stroked her senses, that voice of his like black velvet against the most hidden part of her. And then he began to flood her with pleasure, suckling and teasing and loving.

She wanted to plead with him to finish, but something kept her silent. Perhaps it was an awareness that tonight, Alexandre needed to claim her *his* way—a way that was untamed and utterly without boundaries. Maybe she should've been afraid of such a claiming, fearful that he'd take everything she had and leave her desolate—but she hungered for it, hungered to give him what he needed.

The first tumble into the maelstrom of erotic pleasure caught her unawares. One moment she was drowning in sensation and the next, wild shocks rocketed through her body, squeezing a scream from her throat and causing a volcano of heat in her core.

Opening her eyes, she fought to stay on her feet. Alexandre stood up behind her, his arms keeping her upright. Shifting her hair to one side, he nibbled at her neck, one big hand smoothing its way up her body to cradle a breast.

"Alexandre," she murmured, too sexually sated to be anything less than totally giving, totally his.

Instead of answering, one of his roving hands dropped lower, into her damp curls. The sudden shock of heat was a surprise—she hadn't believed her body could feel anymore. But as Alexandre kissed her neck, one hand teasing at her nipples while the other spread through her intimately, she found she'd been wrong. Desire tore at her, making her lose what breath she'd managed to catch.

She rubbed her face along his sleeve. His shirt was soft against her cheek, the scent of him locked in the fibers. "You're making me melt," she confessed, even as she felt another release approaching. It was an affectionate whisper.

He continued to nibble on the highly vulnerable skin above her pulse. "Again, kitten." It was barely a sound in the darkness, so husky the words were almost lost.

The impact of her second orgasm hit her as hard as the first. But instead of a shocking inferno, this one was a slumbering fire that continued to rage when she'd thought it would flare and burn her out. Alexandre's fingers kept working their magic and she kept tumbling over and over into the smoldering heat. Lights flickered inside her closed lids as she moved her body on his fingers, seeking more of the drug he'd addicted her to.

He gave her what she wanted. More and more and more, until her body was so limp that the aftershocks racing through her only made her moan, too weak to do anything else. Alexandre shifted and suddenly she was in his arms, heading toward the cottage.

Looking down into Charlotte's eyes, Alexandre was lost. He'd wanted to take her out there, under the night sky, but something primitive and possessive in him refused to subject her to the hard earth. Protecting Charlotte was already so much a part of him that he didn't even acknowledge it as an impulse. It just *was*. Pushing through the open door of the cottage, he kicked it shut behind him.

The beacon of light that was her bedroom drew him. Charlotte didn't say a word, rubbing her face against his chest, her arms around his neck. There was such complete acceptance in her that he was humbled, the tyrant in him soothed by her willingness to give him everything he needed. When he lay her down on the bed, she raised her arms. He went to her on a husky groan, covering her body with his.

Under his hands, her skin was smooth, honey-golden and warm. "I love the way you feel, *ma petite*," he murmured, licking the shell of her ear. "The way you move." Kissing his way across her jaw, he suckled her lower lip into his mouth. "The way you taste."

She shivered and whispered something he didn't catch. He just knew she wasn't saying no. Rubbing his face against her neck, he breathed in the scent of her, aware of her fingers threading through his hair. When he nuzzled his way down to her breasts, those graceful hands clenched in expectation. A smile on his lips, he brushed a soft kiss over the slope of one lush breast.

Under him, she squirmed. "Alexandre."

Chuckling, he moved his head and took her nipple into his mouth, having already learned what she ached for. The taste of her sent his senses spinning, drawing him into a vortex of desperate need that he couldn't fight, didn't even want to fight. Under him, her body arched, sensuous and compelling.

Hands on her rib cage, he held her still as he indulged in her. Her other breast tasted as beautiful as the first. A taste wasn't enough. Sucking hard, he held the taut morsel in his mouth while her fingers moved restlessly through his hair to grip his shoulders. He could feel her heart thudding in her chest, rapid and furious.

Then she whispered his name and his hunger became voracious. "I need to be in you." He rose over her.

Her eyes seemed to darken even further as her hands slipped from his hair and down to his belt. He let her get rid of the belt and unzip him. When she closed her hand over his length, he came close to shattering.

Somehow finding the strength, he pulled away only far enough to ensure her protection. Returning, he wrapped her legs around him and nudged at her with his pulsing arousal. Regret that he couldn't feel the silk of her skin through his trousers and shirt tempted him to stop and remove his clothes. Then the ravenous need he had for her grabbed him by the throat and retreat was no longer an option.

Proving her sensuous nature, Charlotte playfully slipped a finger into his mouth, permission for a dance he'd never take by force, no matter his urgency. Suckling at the offering, he pushed into her body in one heavy stroke. Tight, her muscles resisted at first and then pulled him into melting heat and sheer pleasure. Her finger slid out of his mouth, her hands going to clutch at his shoulders, her hands strong despite their apparent fragility.

With her body clenched around him, Alexandre had no ability to think. Glancing at her passion-drenched face to ensure that this was giving her as much pleasure as it was him, he let the final rein slip from his hand and surrendered to the firestorm. Around him, her body was sleek and giving, a perfect fit.

An absolutely perfect fit.

Charlotte Ashton had been made for Alexandre Dupree, was his last thought before his release hit him hard and low, powerful enough to have him seeing sparks. And then Charlotte moved under him and he realized that ecstasy could multiply until there was nothing but sensation sizzling over his skin and shooting through his bloodstream.

He surfaced to find his face buried against the curve of his lover's warm neck, his body cushioned by hers while they remained very intimately connected. Not wanting to leave, he licked at her skin. She shivered.

"Do you want me to move, *ma petite?*" He liked the feel of her silky soft body crushed under his.

She nuzzled him. "No. But could you take off your shirt? The buttons…"

She didn't have to say any more. He realized they had to be pressing into her skin. Barely rising off her, he said, "Undo them."

"You like giving orders too much," she grumbled, but her lips were trying not to smile. Her fingers undid every single button and he shrugged it off. "What about the rest of your clothes?" she said, when he settled back over her.

"To remove them I'd have to withdraw from you. I don't want to."

He felt her blush through the fine skin of the breasts pressed against him. "You were speaking to me in French while we…"

He allowed himself to luxuriate in her body, rolling the exotic scent of her in his mouth. "*Oui,* it's my native tongue. Did you not like it?"

"You know very well I liked it. I just want to know what it meant." Her arms were around his shoulders, lazily stroking.

Content, he lay there and let her pet him, the driving hunger in him calmed by her unconditional giving. "My words would make you blush."

Her lips parted softly at the roughness in his tone and the primitive in him punched to the surface. Leaning close, he began to whisper translations of his more intimate whispers.

"Alexandre!"

Looking down into her scandalized face, he broke out into a smile. "Is this the same woman who stood so proudly naked under the stars only minutes ago?"

Alexandre's sensual voice threatened to make Charlotte lose her train of thought. "Why?" she asked.

"Why?" He gave her a quizzical look.

"Why were you so edgy tonight?"

The skin of his face tightened. "I'm not ready to tell you that."

"You can't keep your secrets forever."

"*Non,*" he agreed. "But I'll keep them for tonight."

Alerted by something in his tone, she kissed him gently. "I know about commitment and loyalty."

He didn't respond with words but she knew he'd heard. For now, it was enough.

After that night, Alexandre's attitude toward her changed. He was no less tender, no less careful with her body, but there was a proprietary hunger in his eyes that stunned her each time he looked at her. And his touch… It made her shiver to think of the sheer possessiveness in it. Spending nights in his arms had become more than an indulgence—it was now a necessity.

But the nights were not all they had, she thought with a smile. Somehow, despite their schedules, they'd managed to sneak away for rides to San Pablo Bay and dinners in the nearby town of Sonoma. There'd also been a repeat of that magical moonlit picnic. It hardly seemed possible that she'd only known him for just under two weeks.

With every moment she spent with him, her sense of rightness grew. Nothing had ever felt as perfect as they did together. Nobody had ever made her dreams come true as he did. When she was with him, she even managed to forget about the envelope from the vital records office that she waited for every single day.

Part of her was glad it had been somehow delayed, giving her a few more precious days to pretend that her mother was alive. But another part of her wanted the truth so badly that sometimes, her whole body hurt. Hurt that only Alexandre's loving could diffuse.

Humming under her breath, she dethorned a long-stemmed rose in preparation for its use in an arrangement. How was it that a sophisticated way-out-of-her-league Frenchman knew her so well, so perfectly?

Perfectly.

Like a mental gunshot, that single word triggered an unexpected and awful train of thought. It was as if her subconscious had been waiting for the dam of her conscious mind to break, allowing the flood of information to roar through her like a river of betrayal.

Her hand stilled. Last night's loving under the starlight had been perfect. It hadn't been similar to what she'd fantasized about, it had been perfect. And before that—the picnics, the dancing, the romance—it had all been perfect, down to the last detail. Her mouth dried up as a horrible suspicion reared its head. The rose dropped from her hand. It couldn't be possible, she argued, how could Alexandre have read her journal?

Her thoughts raced back to the day he'd given her the bouquet, the day she'd found him standing outside the greenhouse. It was feasible that he'd gone searching for her and run across her journal. That day, she'd argued against her instincts, telling herself she was being paranoid. But what if she hadn't been wrong about the knowledge in his eyes? Her hand clasped the stem of another rose. Thorns stabbed into her palm. Wincing, she drew it away, blotted off the tiny pinpricks of blood and resumed dethorning.

It was useless. Her mind continued to circle around the almost certain knowledge that Alexandre had invaded her privacy. More than that, by never owning up to what he'd done, he'd cheated the faith she'd placed in him. Throwing down the flowers, she stalked out to her bike. The ride should've calmed her down but with every moment that passed, she became more and more convinced of the rightness of her suspicion.

Humiliation and anger burned in her cheeks, pain throbbed in her heart. She'd trusted him absolutely and all this time, it had just been a game to him. God, how he must've laughed to discover that in her fantasies, quiet Charlotte Ashton imagined herself a temptress. Tears threatened but she fought them off with fury.

She headed straight to the winery, ignoring the beauty of the spring-green vineyards lit by the late afternoon sun. Alexandre was standing by the steps leading down to the cellar, head bent and face set in thoughtful lines as he spoke to an assistant winemaker. As soon as she entered, his head came up, almost as if he'd scented her presence.

A smile dawned on his handsome face. For once, it didn't immediately soften her heart. She gathered up all her fury, all her anger and waited for him to come to her.

"*Ma chérie,*" he began.

"I need to talk to you. Privately." Without another word, she left the winery and headed toward the vineyard, his prowling presence a dark shadow at her back. The second they were out of hearing range, she whirled.

His expression was wary. "You're angry."

"Yes." She could find no subtle way to ask this. "Did you read my journal?" It came out as a blunt demand.

The lines around his mouth went white. "Yes."

She'd expected anything but that, expected him to offer excuses before he admitted it. "You aren't even going to try and deny it?"

"*Non.* I did read your journal."

Frustrated, she cried, "How could you do that to me? Invade my privacy that way?"

"I didn't plan to do so. But when the opportunity presented itself, I wasn't strong enough to resist." He didn't attempt to touch her, as if aware how thin her control was.

"Well you should have." She clenched her fists. "They were private thoughts, private dreams. You had no right to read them." No right to see the side of herself that she'd never allowed anyone to see. Except him. She'd trusted him and it had been based on a lie. "How would you have liked it if I'd done the same to you?"

His shoulders tightened under the deep green shirt he wore. "Charlotte, you're so self-contained, so protective of your thoughts that I feared I'd never get to know you if I didn't take the chance when it came."

"That's your justification?"

He shook his head, remorse in his eyes. "No. That's simply the reason I told myself it was permissible."

His acceptance of guilt was driving her insane. "You think I'm protective of my thoughts? What about you? You've got a layer of charm that's more impenetrable than steel."

"I've told you things I've never shared with anyone," he said quietly.

She was too distraught to hear the depth of emotion in his tone, too angry to have paid heed to it even if she had heard. "Was this all just a game to you? Seduce the little Indian gardener in your free time?"

Those bitter chocolate eyes darkened to thunder. "I would stop before you go too far." His tone had turned silky, terrifyingly calm.

"Why the hell should I?" She fought the urge to cry— if she broke down in front of him, it would complete her humiliation. "You've had a good laugh at my expense. Well the laugh is over. We're over."

He touched her for the first time, capturing her chin between his forefinger and thumb. "Don't speak so in anger, *ma petite.*"

She jerked her chin away and began to move back. "I mean every word I say. I should be glad you've made it easy for me to break it off—I was beginning to worry that you thought there might be more between us than sex." The lie almost killed her.

For a second, she thought she saw Alexandre's body tremble as if he'd been hit with a hard blow. But when she looked into his eyes, his gaze was blank. It infuriated her that he could remain so calm while her heart was being torn to pieces.

"Now I don't have to worry about breaking your lying heart," she whispered. "Thanks for letting me practice on you—you went way beyond the call of duty. Next time a man seduces me, I'm sure he'll be happy with my skills."

She didn't wait for him to respond. Barely able to see through the haze of fury and pain blinding her, she ran to her bike. It was only as she was riding away that she realized Alexandre had made no effort to follow her.

Eleven

Alexandre lay awake late that night, Charlotte's words slicing through him like sharp knives. Her rejection was all the more terrible because he'd told her things he'd *never* shared with anyone, letting her glimpse the forces that had shaped his soul.

And yet she'd rejected him with such absolute force that he couldn't convince himself she hadn't meant every word. Had she truly been "practicing" on him, using him because he was available? The idea dealt a vicious blow to his inherent masculinity.

Turning, he punched the pillow into shape and tried to forget the incredible anger in her eyes as she'd walked away. He'd misjudged her badly when he'd thought her a woman of too much heart. If she'd been what he'd imagined, she'd never have hurt him so.

He knew he should forget her and move on but that was proving impossible. Adoring her had become as vital to him as breathing. How could he have been so wrong about her, so mistaken as to her nature?

Suddenly, he recalled one of the very first entries in her journal.

...for me, this act is more than bodies meeting, more than simple pleasure, more than just the physical...

She'd asked him how he would've felt if she'd invaded his privacy. In all honesty, he would've been furious—furious enough to do and say far worse things than she had in that flaring burst of anger and hurt—he'd wounded the woman he so desperately needed to protect and been so blinded by his own pain that he hadn't seen hers.

Cursing his stupidity, he got out of bed. The temptation to go to Charlotte and ask her forgiveness was hard to resist. Despite her anger, he knew she was too gentle to make him beg, knew that she'd forgive him the second she heard the sincerity in his tone and that was why he couldn't take that road. It would be too easy and her hurt deserved proper recompense.

He'd been arrogant in reading her private thoughts but he couldn't regret it, not when it had brought him Charlotte. Sweet Charlotte with her tenderness and her hope and her caring. Now she was feeling violated and betrayed by the man she'd trusted with her innocence.

He couldn't stand knowing that, couldn't bear to let the woman who'd given him flowers think that she was in any way lesser in their dance because he'd seen the sensual heart of her. To do that, he had to make her understand what he'd felt when he'd read her thoughts. And he knew only one way to do that.

Even as he began an apology that laid his soul bare, he shied away from the reason behind his driving need to lessen Charlotte's hurt. He wasn't yet ready to face that powerful feeling, not yet willing to accept how hard he'd fallen for a woman whose smile alone could destroy him.

* * *

Charlotte awoke later than usual, courtesy of a sleepless night. Guilt hadn't made a good bed-companion. Notwithstanding his own actions, she knew she'd hurt Alexandre and accepted that he deserved an apology. However, she hadn't been able to screw up the courage last night. Would he even listen? He was so proud under that charming sophistication, so conscious of his past that her horrible words would've wounded him terribly.

She'd tried to convince herself that of course he wouldn't believe what she'd said. Of course he'd know that for her, making love with a man meant something far more than physical pleasure. After all, he'd been privy to her innermost thoughts.

But she hadn't been able to rest easy, too conscious of the fact that in spite of his strength, Alexandre had deep vulnerabilities. Vulnerabilities such as those fostered by his father's implied rejection and his mother's lifestyle choice.

Deep inside, her beautiful, sensual Alexandre didn't believe he was good enough for love and loyalty. Her reckless words would've further cemented that impression. She'd said she'd been practicing on him! The recollection made her cringe. No, she couldn't let him think that he'd only been a convenience. Never could she let the man who'd shown her such tenderness think that.

Taking a deep, fortifying breath, she opened the cottage door. Her intention to go to him turned into panic when she saw the white envelope that lay on her doorstep, weighted down by a rock. What if he'd taken her words at face value and decided to break off all ties? Picking up the envelope with trembling hands, she retreated inside.

The envelope contained several sheets of paper covered

with words written in a strong, flowing hand. Hoping desperately that this wasn't what she thought, she forced herself to read.

Lover mine,...

Disbelieving, she collapsed in a nearby armchair. Surely, surely, Alexandre couldn't have done this, couldn't have given her this surrender after the way she'd hurt him?

And yet he had.

Proud, elegant, intensely private Alexandre Dupree had given her access to his most secret thoughts, his most secret fantasies.

She lowered her eyes to the page.

Lover mine,

You ask me for my fantasies, for my dreams. Yet will you believe me when I say that you are my ultimate fantasy, a woman of fire and beauty, spirit and soul, breathtaking sensuality and heartbreaking tenderness?

Your smile can bring me to my knees. Your touch leaves me at your mercy. Ah, *ma chérie,* would that you'd be satisfied with that and ask for nothing more. But I know you have a right to demand the same openness from me that I forced onto you. For a man who's spent a lifetime keeping secrets, it's a difficult thing to do. Difficult, not impossible.

So what do I dream of my Charlotte doing to me? What makes me wake hard and aching for you? What makes me sweat even on the coldest night?

Let me tell you, kitten.

Inside her chest, Charlotte's heart was thumping at what felt like a thousand beats a second.

In my fantasies, it's always night and we're always behind closed doors. I'm not a man who likes to share you, though you know too well that sometimes I can't control the urge to possess you wherever you might be. And ever since that night outside your cottage (*merci, ma petite*), taking you under the starry sky has become one of my favorite erotic fantasies.

Charlotte licked her lips, a small smile edging her lips at the memory of the hunger in him that night. She should've realized right then and there that this was no game for either of them. Lifting her hair off her suddenly heated nape, she continued to read.

In my dreams, you're dressed in something that I'm sure would make you blush, but a man is allowed to take liberties in his fantasies and if they lead to strips of white lace and ribbon, well, I can only enjoy the sight.

White lace and ribbon?

Your clothing is so fine, so delicate, that it entices rather than hides, the silk curtain of your hair reflecting the flames in the fireplace by which you stand. Did I forget to tell you that we are in my chalet in Switzerland, snowed in?

The fire is to keep our bodies warm but I don't need its aid when you're standing there, looking at me like you'd like nothing better than to strip me naked and lick every inch of my skin.

Charlotte blinked and took a deep breath. Sometimes, that was exactly what she wanted to do to her charming lover with his too-sexy body and masculine beauty. She'd never admitted the scandalous desire.

> I confess that I'd enjoy being caressed so by you, being seduced by each slow flick of your tongue. But, I can wait until you're ready to give me such loving.
>
> In this fantasy, you undress me and then my dear, sweet, Charlotte, you touch me with hands that know I'm yours, utterly and completely. You tug me to face the fireplace and sink to your knees in front of me on the creamy sheepskin rug by the hearth. I ache for the touch of your lips, the temptation of your mouth, the heated torture of your slow loving.
>
> Smiling, you give me what I desire.

Charlotte stopped breathing. He was making her toes curl, making her want to give him everything he'd fantasized about. Her eyes widened. Was this what he'd felt when he'd read her journal? This need to fulfill his fantasies had nothing to do with power or being in control and everything to do with pleasing him—giving the man she loved exactly what he needed.

Her hand clenched on the page. *The man she loved.* She blinked and took a deep breath. Well, at least that explained why she'd acted so badly yesterday. In spite of her attempts to the contrary, she'd fallen soul-deep in love with the man. What was she going to do?

The decision was far easier than she'd thought it would be. He'd never lied to her about his intentions. Though he felt more for her than she'd ever believed he would, he was going to leave her one day soon. All she could do was love him for as long as she could.

Shoving aside the incipient pain, she focused instead on the depth of commitment implied by the words he'd written.

By the time she finished reading, her face was flushed and she knew a few things she hadn't before. Best of all, she knew that she was the only lover Alexandre thought capable of fulfilling his most scorching fantasies. Some of her earlier sorrow dissipated at the realization, and she let herself be drawn fully into his world.

The man had sensual eroticism in his blood. With nothing more than his words, he'd seduced her. And with his final confession, he'd conquered more than her body, he'd stolen the last pieces of her heart.

All this and more, I'd like you to do to me, *ma chérie*, but my deepest fantasy, the one I'd most like fulfilled, is to be allowed to fulfill every one of yours. Nothing pleases me more than your pleasure. Nothing.

Forgive me for any hurt I caused you, Charlotte and let me adore you as I ache to do.

Alexandre hadn't been able to concentrate on anything since the moment he'd left the letter on Charlotte's doorstep. It was just as well that the work that had originally brought him to the estate was almost complete.

"I've helped you as far as I can," he told Trace, as they stood outside the winery. "There is only so much that I can do in the short time I'm here, particularly given that you're not currently processing the harvest.

"I can point out areas of improvement and suggest strategies, but to build a reputation as a premier winemaker, you must devote long-term attention to every step of the process."

"Beginning with the grapes themselves," Trace said, a touch of humor in his tone. "Inferior, mass-produced grapes equal inferior mass-produced wine."

"Ah, I see I've beaten you over the head with that particular point too many times." Alexandre smiled but his heart wasn't in it. Where was Charlotte? Had he ripped open his soul and still been unable to win her back? What would he do if she didn't forgive him?

"James and his assistants are good at what they do," he continued, "but you need to hire someone whose goal is not mass production, but fostering distinctiveness—someone who isn't afraid to experiment and innovate. One team can't do both and produce great wines, not given the scale of this vineyard and your production levels."

"Are you happy to keep consulting for us?"

What if he'd lost Charlotte forever? Would he want to return to this place that held so many memories? "I will, of course, provide several reports arising from this visit, but beyond that, I can't promise anything. You're welcome to contact me and if the timing suits…" He shrugged.

"Can I try to make you an offer you can't refuse?"

Alexandre looked into the man's intelligent face. "You couldn't make me such an offer."

Trace gave a good-natured nod. Before he left to walk back into the winery, he hesitated and then said, "I know you've been seeing Charlotte. I just want to say I've never seen her happier. Good luck sorting out whatever it is that's happened."

Alexandre knew he'd need more than luck. Charlotte had to be feeling betrayed and hurt, and more than anything else, that tore at him. Fists clenched in his pockets, he decided to walk off some of his excess energy. He wouldn't push Charlotte, even though he was dying every moment that she didn't give him an answer. Shoulders set, he'd taken no more than three steps when his cell phone rang.

Frowning, he pulled it out of his pocket. His frustration disappeared the second he saw the caller ID. "Charlotte."

A pause. "Are you free to come to the cottage?"

"*Oui.* I can be there in a few minutes."

"Well…I'll see you then."

Alexandre hung up and walked to the golf cart some-one had parked by the winery, his jaw clenched. Charlotte's tone of voice had given nothing away. He wondered if she'd asked him over to tell him his letter meant nothing to her. His fingers tightened painfully on the wheel of the vehicle he'd commandeered.

Charlotte opened the door the second she heard Alexandre arrive. As she watched him cross the short distance between them, she rubbed her palms on her wraparound skirt, her heart beating triple time. Could she really do this? Trust this man so much?

He reached her, those dark French eyes coolly emotionless. Not so long ago, his calm elegance would've intimidated her. Now, she thought wonderingly, she could see beneath the surface and the man she saw had her heart tumbling. There was a strange vulnerability about Alexandre, and suddenly, she knew that he thought she was going to mock his confession and reject him.

And yet he'd come.

"Good morning," she murmured.

"Is it?" His voice was rough, husky.

Tugging at his hands, she pulled him inside and shut the door. "Mine started out very nicely."

His lips curled faintly upward. "And why was that, *ma petite?*"

She hadn't been aware that she'd been waiting for the endearment. Putting her hands on his chest, she leaned in close. "I discovered that a gorgeous hunk of a man finds me irresistible." A flush streaked his cheeks. Her eyes widened. "You're embarrassed!"

"*Non,*" he refuted, scowling at her. "Alexandre Dupree doesn't get embarrassed."

It touched her that her compliment had done this to her urbane lover. More importantly, it gave her the courage to propose what she was about to. "Do you have to be back at the winery soon?"

"*Non.* All the practical work is done. I have to write a few reports but that can be done anytime within a month. There is no urgency."

Her heart slumped. So soon, he'd be gone. But, she decided, she wouldn't think about that, not now. If this was all she was ever going to have of the man she loved, then she'd take hold of it with both hands. "I'm so sorry about what I said. I didn't mean any of it."

"It is forgotten." There was no recrimination in his tone, nothing but tenderness.

Taking a deep breath, she asked, "Would you like to spend the day with me?"

His expression softened in a way that she knew was for her alone. "Of course. What would you like to do? We can go for a drive if you wish."

She shook her head. "I have another idea." A scandalous idea, especially since it was bright light outside.

His face was suddenly all male, as if she'd somehow given herself away. "Tell me this idea." Strong arms slipped around her waist, showing her that he was once more certain of his right to touch her, aware that she'd forgiven him.

Swallowing, she fingered a button on his white shirt and looked up into his eyes. "I'd like to make your deepest fantasy come true," she whispered.

Around her his arms firmed. "My deepest fantasy is to love you until you are drunk on your own pleasure." One hand flattened on her lower back, big and hot. His eyes were so intent, she felt devoured.

"I know."

He shuddered and leaned down to brush his lips across

hers. "How can you be so generous after I put tears in your eyes?" His tone was raw.

She heard the sincere regret in his voice. "Because you've also brought a thousand smiles to my heart."

He hugged her to him. "*Ma petite,* you destroy me with your honesty, with your capacity to forgive so much hurt. I promise to never again betray your trust in me."

Shaking her head, she cupped his face in her hands and said, "I understand the temptation you faced—I could no more have stopped reading your letter than I could've stopped breathing."

"*Oui?*"

She fought her blush. "I read every single word. And then I read them over. So, we're even."

The bright joy in his eyes rocked her. "Then, kitten, are you ready to play?"

"Yes."

"Do you know what I wish to do to you the most?"

"What?"

"I wish to love you as you wrote in your journal—a loving that demands submission and absolute trust."

She knew which fantasy he was referring to. "I trust you." Otherwise, she would've never gone into his arms. For her, there was no separating the physical from the emotional. She was his, body and soul.

Charlotte found herself facing Alexandre behind the locked doors of her bedroom. With the curtain pulled, daylight barely filtered through, creating an intimate darkness that caused desire to uncurl luxuriously within her body. It also lent a scandalous edge to this already wicked rendezvous.

In bare feet, Alexandre padded across the carpet to her. Without her own shoes, she felt even smaller against his compelling masculinity. But not in any way less of a woman. Alexandre liked her size, she thought, smiling inside. Every time he called her *ma petite* in that seducer's voice of his, he told her just how much he appreciated the woman she was.

"Are you sure?" Alexandre touched her cheek with a finger, his eyes lingering on her face.

Taking hold of his hand, she kissed the tip of that finger. *"Oui."*

At the teasing acquiescence, his face lit from within. That brilliance held something far more potent than lust, but she didn't want to question just what it was that she'd seen, didn't want to give herself false hope. Not now, not in this moment of utter truth between them.

He unclipped the single barrette she'd used to hold her hair back. Dropping it to the floor, he ran the strands through his fingers, letting them fall across her chest. The backs of his hands brushed her breasts as he played with her hair and she sucked in a breath at the sudden sensual heat.

Moving back, he raised dark eyes to her face. "Take off your clothes for me, Charlotte."

It was a gentle command, but a command nonetheless. Just as she'd asked for in her most shocking fantasy. Hands trembling with a combination of desire and nerves, she raised them to the bottom of her white top. It was simply fashioned, with a scoop neck and cap sleeves, but its magic lay in the way it shaped her body, following each curve with smooth perfection.

Without taking her eyes from his, she began to raise the material, arms crossed across her front. Heat sparked to life in the darkness of Alexandre's gaze as an inch of flesh was revealed, and suddenly she had all the confidence she needed.

She pulled the top off in a swift motion. It left her standing before him in a white lace bra and a knee-length skirt that wrapped around her like a sarong. When he continued to simply watch, she moved her hands to the side tie of the skirt and undid it. Her nerves returned and she held the two undone halves closed, unable to move her hands and drop the skirt.

As if he'd heard her unspoken plea, Alexandre whispered, "You are so lovely…take off your skirt for me. I hunger to see all that glorious golden skin of yours."

Swallowing at the molten heat in his gaze, she took the ends of the tie and unwrapped the skirt. Her hair swung in front of her as she dropped her head to watch the cool blue material puddle on the floor, a blatant exclamation mark of surrender.

When she raised her head, silken strands settled back over her lace-covered breasts. A little self-conscious, she didn't know what to do with her hands. Aware that her lacy underwear didn't hide much, she was tempted to cover herself but that would be cheating.

Walking to her, Alexandre took hold of her hands and gently placed them behind her back, playfully manacling them with one strong hand. With his other, he swept the concealing wings of her hair behind her back, so that her chest was shielded only by delicate white lace.

He looked at her for so long, her entire body flushed. "Tell me, Charlotte." He rubbed his thumb across one peaked nipple. She jerked. "Tell me why you're dressed so seductively." He lifted his head, that beautiful mahogany hair falling across his forehead.

No room to hide. Licking her lips, she said, "I wanted to be…luscious for you." Her voice was hoarse, her throat dry with anticipation.

One hand closed over her breast, molding and shaping. Something in his careful touch screamed possessiveness.

"*Merci, ma petite.* You are exquisite." Looking straight into her eyes, he asked, "How far?"

Her heart was beating in her throat. "As far as you wish," she said, giving him total control.

Twelve

Alexandre kissed her, his hand still on her breast. When she attempted to deepen the kiss, he pulled away. Frustrated, her body continued to press against his.

He released her. "Get on the bed for me, kitten."

Warmth coalescing in her stomach, she did as he asked, sitting on her knees with her back to him. Looking over her shoulder, she asked, "Is this okay?"

The maleness in his eyes sent shivers up her spine, the tiny hairs on her body standing up in attention. This fantasy was far more potent than she'd imagined, far more emotionally involved. As a woman, she was putting her body and her mind in his hands, to hurt or to pleasure.

That led to the inescapable conclusion that she would've only taken this step if she was certain of his nature, sure that he was a man who'd always choose to pleasure, never to harm.

"*Non*. Face me."

She turned, still on her knees.

"Brush your hair away for me."

Raising her hands, she moved her hair to her back, feeling the slide of it against her skin. It was suddenly erotic after a lifetime of being unnoticed. "Like this?"

"*Oui*. Put your hands flat on your thighs." The command held a rough edge, as if keeping his distance was torture.

She was suddenly aware that he'd placed her like a prize in the middle of the bed. "Now what?"

He smiled at her, slow and pleased. "Now you watch."

He undid the first button on his dusty-blue shirt. The heat in her stomach blazed into roiling flame. She'd never imagined that he'd pleasure her like this. So very masculine, control came easily to him, but this teasing show told her that he was comfortable enough in his skin to give her a little surrender. And that was the one thing she'd doubted about his ability to fulfill her fantasy.

Three buttons down, all she could focus on was the dark hair that lightly covered that glowing, healthy wedge of skin. Barely breathing, she watched him undo two more buttons before pulling out the tails of his shirt to complete the job. Leaving the shirt on, he undid his belt buckle and slid the belt out of the loops. Slowly.

Charlotte's body was leaning toward his. She wanted to touch him so badly, her hands began to drift up from her thighs. Alexandre dropped the belt to the floor and said, "*Non, ma chérie*. Place your hands as I asked."

Without a second thought, she obeyed, a thrill racing through her as she remembered her own words. She'd asked for *commands laced with rough tenderness* and Alexandre was delivering. His eyes held the open adoration that she'd dreamed of—confident and proud, he didn't mind letting her see the effect she had on him.

When she put her hands back on her thighs, he said,

"Very good, Charlotte." It was a husky whisper. "I should reward such perfect obedience."

A spark of rebellion appeared in her. "I think you're enjoying this too much."

He shrugged off his shirt, revealing an upper body as beautiful as any Greek god's. However, his grin could've done justice to the most wicked of devils. "*Oui,* of course. I have a beautiful woman half-naked and willing to do anything I ask. I would be an idiot not to take advantage."

His sheer delight in the situation had all her simmering outrage disappearing. Wonder took its place—her serious, sophisticated lover was playing with her. This was a game, a sensual, erotic game that could only be played between two lovers who were completely attuned to each other's needs.

He prowled over to her, so gracefully dangerous that her breath caught. When he reached the bed, he placed his hands on her shoulders and leaning over, pressed his lips against hers. Starving for a taste of him, she opened immediately, inviting him with the strokes of her tongue that she knew he liked. Moaning when he returned the caress, she had to clench her hands on her thighs to keep from thrusting them in his hair.

When he drew back from her, she wanted to whimper in disappointment. His eyes were dark ebony, glittering night. "The taste of you is like some forbidden drug."

In my fantasies, you are strong enough...to openly adore my body without seeing it as a weakness.

Charlotte wondered how fate could've sent her a lover so perfect. She knew him well enough to understand that this was no pretence, not merely an attempt to deliver her fantasy. To him, she was beautiful—a potent drug. What woman could resist such a lover?

Alexandre's attention suddenly shifted to something

over her shoulder. Unable to turn, she waited, nerves taut, as he walked around the double bed. After what seemed like an endless moment, the mattress depressed behind her.

His first touch made her shiver. Chuckling, he swept her hair over one shoulder, leaving her back bare to him. His lips brushed her nape.

"Alexandre," she couldn't help moaning.

Then he was gone and she felt the stroke of something unutterably soft against her skin, tantalizing and luxurious. After one melting stroke, warm breath whispered across the spot. Her entire body jolted into sensory overload. Alexandre repeated the action on her lower back and her whimper was of sheer pleasure.

One big hand slid around to lay flat against her belly, but before she could concentrate on that feeling, strong male teeth scraped lightly along her lower back, just above the swell of her bottom.

Alexandre felt Charlotte jerk, her stomach going taut under his hand. When he repeated the caress, a sheen of perspiration broke out over her skin. Her beauty continued to astound him. She was like a cool, clear lake, but one with unexpected depths, soul-deep loveliness hidden beneath the gentle outer layer.

Breathing in the intoxicating scent of her, he kissed his way up her spine until he knelt behind her once more. This time he put both arms around her waist. When she saw the feather he held in his hand, she laughed. "So that's what you were torturing me with."

"It was very accommodating of you to have a vase full of feathers for my use," he teased, dropping the feather so he could touch her skin more fully as he kissed the bared curve of her neck.

Sliding his hands up and down her arms, he gently massaged her, indulging himself with the feel of her skin. She

sighed and leaned into his body, her bare back coming into contact with his chest. Both of them reacted to the skin
to skin touch, but which one of them gasped, Alexandre
couldn't tell.

"Will you move your hands to your sides?" he asked.

"Yes."

Unable to believe how much she trusted him, delight-
fully shocked by this strong woman who didn't always
need to be in control with her man, he wanted to give her
everything. Slipping his hands between her ribs and her
arms, he spread his palms on her thighs where her hands
had rested. Fine tremors shook her body as he moved his
fingers along the sensitive inner faces.

Barely brushing the lace protecting her, he moved both
hands up her body. Her moan had blood flooding to his already pounding erection. Breath labored, he moved his
hands over her torso, warm and so soft, and cupped her
lace-covered breasts.

He could tell she was fighting the urge to touch him. The
fact that he tempted her just as much as she tempted him
was an aphrodisiac greater than anything else on this earth.
She fit perfectly in his hands, the high, taut fruit of her
breasts shaped for him alone.

Closing his hands, he touched skin where the lace of her
bra ended. Continuing to lave her neck with kisses, he began to massage her sensitive flesh. Her body arched toward
his and the hands she held at her sides curled into fists and
finally, clenched on his thighs, which he'd spread to cradle her body back into his.

He chuckled, riding the wave of desire threatening to
swamp him. "You're cheating."

Under his hands, her breasts moved up and down as she
gasped for breath. "Maybe you should just tie me up next
time."

His breath caught. "I'll use silk scarves," he promised. "But, this time, I'll let you get away with it."

She laughed, the sound an intimate caress in the semi-light of the room. "You're making me…*melt*."

He wanted nothing more than to thrust into her melting heat, but this fantasy of theirs wasn't finished. Not by a long shot. He began to play with her breasts in earnest, feeling the cool slide of her hair against the back of one hand, a double sensory temptation.

Her body moved against his, sinuously rubbing his erection until his heartbeat was concentrated in that one spot, hot and hard. Feeling sweat break out on his back, he withdrew his hands, dropping them to lie on her hips.

"Alexandre," she moaned, turning her head to give him a reproachful look.

"Take off your bra, kitten." His voice was so rough, he wondered if she understood him.

But she did. Turning away, she reached behind her back, her knuckles sliding against his skin. Sucking in a breath, he said, "Behave."

He felt her smile in the way her body relaxed into his. Then she pulled away and unhooked the back catch of her bra. Moving her hands to her front, she peeled it off, holding the scrap of satin and lace for a second before throwing it to the floor.

He couldn't see her breasts yet, but the glorious honey-colored sweep of her back was open to his gaze. Murmuring his appreciation to her in his native tongue, he stroked that dusky-gold skin with both hands. Some of the words were spoken against her skin as he kissed his way across her shoulders, his hands stroking over her waist.

Her body relaxed into him. With a slight shift, he ensured that their bodies pressed together, temptation and torture for both of them. Hooking his left arm around her waist after ensuring her silky hair wasn't caught between, he whispered, "Lean over my arm."

Without pause, she obeyed the husky order. He cradled her slight weight easily as she arched, her lovely face looking up into his. All her hair slid off, baring her to him. As his free hand stroked up her stomach to close over a breast, he lowered his lips to sip from hers. A sip led to a deeper caress as he delved into her mouth.

Under his stroking hand, her flesh was taut and sheened with sweat, her heartbeat thudding against his fingertips. As he kissed her, he rolled a nipple between his fingertips. Her whole body jerked.

"Alexandre…I can't…" she moaned as he repeated the caress on her other breast.

"Shhh, kitten, take just a little more," he coaxed, sliding his hand from her breasts to the heat between her legs. Teasing them both, he ran his fingers along the top edges of her lacy underwear.

He was so aroused it was almost painful and yet he didn't want to end this delicious game of the senses. Carefully, watching her dark eyes go even darker, he slipped his hand under the elastic band to cup her. Her whole body went taut, her pupils dilated and then, fine tremors rocked her entire body.

Masculine satisfaction roared over him as he watched her shatter in his arms. Spreading his fingers, he stroked her softness, delighted when her body arched up and surrendered to another surge of pleasure.

When the last waves had broken within her, he lay her boneless body down on the bed. As she straightened her legs, the scent of heat and musk rose into the air. His nostrils flared, hunger punching to the surface. Moving to position himself between her thighs, he pushed both her legs up until her feet were flat on the bed, knees raised.

Long lashes lifted. "You look very pleased with your-self." Her voice held the tones of a woman who had been well-pleasured.

He dropped his head and pressed a kiss to the warm skin of her navel, breathing in the scent of her. "Are you pleased with me, Charlotte?"

"Oh, yes," she murmured.

Aching for relief, Alexandre knew he had to have a taste of her before he stormed her body. He kissed his way down her stomach, not stopping the caresses when he met the fine barrier of satin and lace. Surprised, she cried out, her sen-sitized flesh feeling too much, even through the fragile silky covering.

Cradling her bottom in his hands, he lifted her to his mouth, loving her through the damp material. Her cries urged him to lave pleasure upon pleasure as she lay spread out for his delectation. When she gave a tiny scream and started to shudder, he finally lifted his head, looking down at the lushness of her. He'd turned the satin and lace sheer, but even that silken shield was too much now.

His hunger was such that he almost tore them off, but at the last moment, he remembered that this was the ful-fillment of a fantasy. "Take off your panties for me," he whispered in her ear.

Dazed eyes met his. "Alexandre?"

He kissed her, rubbing his body against the length of hers, feeling her softness and her melting welcome. "Will you take them off for me?"

She barely nodded. He lifted off her and she reached down and moved her body just enough to slip the scrap of lace to her thighs. It seemed beyond her to push them down her legs.

He reached out and helped her until she lay naked and golden below him. Shuddering, he stroked her thighs. "If

you didn't look so satisfied lying there, I'd order you to finish undressing me," he whispered, well aware that he'd
never last if she took on the job.

Her eyes widened. She licked her lips. "I think my
strength is coming back to me."

"No touching this time." He decided to save that torture
for another loving. Moving off the bed, he stripped his
pants and underwear off with brutal efficiency, aware of her
eyes eating him up. She didn't look away when he took
care of protection, pure possession in her gaze.

When he settled back between her thighs, there was only welcome in every part of her, from her desire-blind eyes
to her passion-warm body. "Shall I take you now?"

Her smile was slow. "You can do whatever you like."

Groaning at the way she'd played their game to the end,
he entered her in one solid stroke. Her body held him tight,
all creamy heat and feminine invitation. Hands holding
on to her hips, he moved in and out once before her legs
locked around him.

"Legs down," he managed to say hoarsely.

After a moment's rebellion, she put her feet flat on the
sheets once more. Adoring her for being the woman she
was, he kissed her. Then, using his tongue to mimic the way
his body slid and out of hers, he set a slow but powerful
rhythm that succeeded in driving his woman to one more
peak before his own climax took hold of him, savage and
hot, like white lightning in his bloodstream.

Sometime before four that afternoon, a knock on the
door had Charlotte snapping her head up from the kitchen
table. "Thank goodness I finally got dressed," she muttered. Taking off her apron, she closed the bedroom door,
where Alexandre was dressing after their shower.

She'd escaped first, giggling from his unexpected playfulness under the streaming water. He'd only let her go after extracting a promise of hot coffee and food. Smiling at the memory, she opened the door.

It was Lara, one of the maids up at the estate house. She held out an envelope. "Came in special delivery, so I thought I should bring it down straight away."

Charlotte forced herself to reply through the buzzing in her head. "Thanks, Lara."

"You're welcome." The auburn-haired woman grinned and began to head back to her golf cart. "I better get back to help with dinner."

Charlotte closed the door with trembling hands. She was still standing there staring at the envelope when Alexandre walked out of the bedroom, shirt hanging open over his chest. "*Ma petite,* what is it?"

"It's from Nebraska's vital records office." Her voice sounded eerily calm, even to her own ears.

He nudged her toward the sofa and sat down beside her. Putting his arm around her, he held her as she gathered her thoughts and slit open the envelope. It was immediately clear that it contained only a single copied death certificate.

Heart pounding, she scanned the cover letter. "It apologizes for the delay—they had some trouble locating the certificates as I was unable to give them several required details. But, they're happy to inform me that they were partially successful.

"Enclosed is the death certificate for David Ashton," she read. "However, they're unable to provide one for Mary Little Dove Ashton…they're certain that no such record exists." A sob caught in her throat.

Alexandre pulled her into a gentle hug. "That's good news."

"I'm afraid to hope," she whispered. "What if they made a mistake?"

He didn't point out that the lateness of the response indicated that the records office had tried hard to locate the certificate. "That should be easy enough to check. Let's call the number they've given for further information." He reached behind himself to pick up the cordless phone from the end table.

Charlotte nodded and accepted the phone. Taking a deep breath, she punched in the numbers. An efficient-sounding voice answered. When she told the operator what she needed, she was transferred to the person who'd done the original search. The man double-checked his files.

"Thanks." A few minutes later she hung up the phone and looked at Alexandre. She couldn't seem to stop trembling. "They didn't make a mistake. There's no death certificate for Mary Little Dove Ashton. The clerk even checked under just Little and Dove and Ashton." The words were coming too fast. "If they died in the same accident and my father's certificate is in Nebraska, shouldn't my mother's be as well?"

He tightened his embrace, leaving her only enough freedom to look up at him. "It would make sense that they would both be filed at the same place. So, it says that your father passed away at the hospital in…Kendall?"

She looked at the copy of the certificate again, as if the information might've changed. "Yes. Kendall General Hospital." And suddenly, she knew what Alexandre was saying. "I need to go there. To be sure."

"They might not give you the information."

Her heart shattered at the tenderness in his expression. "We won't need anything more from them than to know if my mother was discharged. I can prove I'm her child with my birth certificate, and if we say she disappeared, they might help us."

Alexandre nodded. "With it being a small-town hospital, they might even know where she went."

Hope leapt in Charlotte's heart but she squelched it. "If she went anywhere at all."

Thirteen

After they'd made the decision to go to Kendall, things moved at breakneck speed. By the end of the day, Alexandre had organized to charter a plane from Napa County Airport to Broken Bow Airport. A rental car would be waiting for them when they arrived in the central Nebraska town. Kendall was around an hour and half drive from Broken Bow and had no suitable airstrip.

Charlotte accepted his help with the organization since she had to juggle her schedule in order to clear the next two days. Given the speed of the sleek twin-engine jet Alexandre had chartered, the round-trip could be done in a day. However, she knew that whatever they found, she'd need at least a day to calm herself.

"We'll leave at seven o'clock tomorrow morning," Alexandre told her as they lay in bed that night. "The jet can get us to Nebraska in under three hours. If all goes well, we should be back here for dinner."

"That plane—it's very expensive, isn't it?"

"Charlotte, I need to do this much for you." His arm tightened. "I can't change the past but I can help you find the truth. Don't reject my gift."

Her heart tumbled over. "How can I, after you said that? Thank you."

Nestling closer to his warm body, she wrapped an arm around his chest, feeling a sharp ache at the sudden thought that far too soon she'd be sleeping alone in this bed. Alone with a broken heart and shattered dreams. Yet, if she had to do it over, she'd take the same road. Loving didn't allow for easy choices.

"I guess we better get some sleep." She knew he'd ascribe her subdued tone to the oncoming trip, but right now, that seemed like a distant dream. Her reality was that soon she'd lose the man she loved. And there was nothing she could do. If all the beauties before her hadn't been able to, what hope did she have of holding a man so emotionally scarred, he didn't trust in love and loyalty?

"Are you sure you wish to rest, *ma petite?*" Alexandre's voice caressed her in the darkness.

She felt a bittersweet smile curve her lips, aware he couldn't see it in the unlit room. "Well, I could be persuaded into a little wakeful activity."

For Charlotte, the early-morning trip to Nebraska passed by in a blur. Alexandre sat with her but didn't attempt to draw her into conversation, as if aware that she needed the time to prepare herself.

When they arrived in Nebraska, she was struck by the dry heat, but her mind was too preoccupied to notice much else. Once they were on the road, her tension transmuted into a kind of nervous excitement that left her so jittery, she felt like she might shatter.

"Stop hurting so much, *ma petite,*" Alexandre ordered after half an hour.

"I can't help it."

He reached across and touched her cheek. Somehow, the simple contact made her feel better than a hundred words could have. For the rest of the drive, his small touches allowed her to gain a measure of peace.

And then they were in Kendall, the last known residence of Mary Little Dove Ashton. The hospital wasn't hard to find, the orange brick facade standing out from a distance. Despite her attempt at curing herself of hope, Charlotte couldn't help her thudding pulse and sweaty palms. Stepping out of the car, she closed her door just as Alexandre rounded the hood and took her hand in his.

"The moment of truth," she whispered, staring ahead at the building that might just change her life.

"Come, *ma chérie,* let's see what they have to tell us. Remember, I'm here with you." *Always.*

Her heart heard the word he couldn't say, haunted by his own demons. But as he was here for her now, she'd be there for him through the tough times. Sooner or later, Alexandre would begin to believe that not all women were fickle and manipulative.

Rebellion spouted inside her, deep and fierce.

Who said their relationship had to end the minute he left the estate? He seemed in no hurry to sever the threads binding them and she refused to let him walk out of her life without a fight. "I'm so glad you're here."

With those simple words, they walked the short distance to the hospital door and entered. The smell of antiseptic, the sound of a crying baby and the clean white walls hit Charlotte all at once.

Her father had died within these walls.

Somehow, she managed to keep herself together even as

that thought whispered through her mind. They went straight to the reception desk manned by a young woman in a crisp nurse's uniform. Her nametag read "Ann Johnson."

"Can I help you?" The nurse glanced up.

"My name is Charlotte Ashton," Charlotte began, taking strength from Alexandre's presence. He didn't try to take over this thing that she had to do, but she knew without a doubt that he'd never let her stumble. "My mother and father were admitted into this hospital almost twenty-two years ago. I was told that they both died."

"I see." Nurse Johnson's eyes had widened and she was giving them her full attention.

"However, when I applied for death certificates, I was told that there was no record of my mother's death."

"How extraordinary. Perhaps there was a mix-up?"

Charlotte couldn't quite pull off a smile. "That's what I'm trying to find out. I need to see my mother's record from all those years ago. Her name was Mary Little Dove Ashton."

"We don't really release that kind of thing." The woman's expression was sympathetic but firm.

"I have proof that she was my mother." Charlotte slid her birth certificate across the counter. "And this is my father's death certificate."

The young nurse appeared undecided.

"Look, you don't have to show us the file. Can you check and tell me if she died here? I just want to know if she…if she lived," she finished softly, unaware how haunted her eyes looked at that moment.

The nurse stood and carefully examined both documents. Finally, she pushed them back at Charlotte. "It's not really procedure but I can't see the harm. Records that far back were never put into the computer system so I'll have to go down to the basement."

Turning, she paged someone over the intercom. "As soon as Jack arrives to man the desk, I'll go down. Let me just copy down the date on your father's death certificate—it'll help me locate the files. I can't promise I'll find the information but I'll try my best."

"Thank you." Charlotte couldn't keep the feeling out of her voice. "Thank you so much."

Alexandre's arm slipped around her shoulders. "Where should we wait for you?" he asked Nurse Johnson.

The woman tucked a strand of blond hair behind her ear. "Just take a seat over there." She pointed to the waiting area. It already had four occupants—an elderly man, a woman with a crying baby and a teenager with a cast on one leg.

Just then, a male nurse arrived to relieve Johnson. Alexandre led Charlotte away from the desk and toward the free chairs in the back of the room. Because of its small size, they remained in close proximity to the woman with the crying baby.

"Oh, hush, honey," the mother coaxed. "The doctor will give you something to stop the hurt." She looked over her shoulder at them. "I'm sorry but he's—"

Alexandre interrupted her. "There's no need for an apology, is there, Charlotte?"

Charlotte blinked awake from the almost trancelike state she'd drifted into. "No, of course not. I hope it's nothing serious?"

"Allergies—nothing so bad, only he's got a rash and the itching's driving him crazy. But the doctor might've found something that'll help."

"I'm glad."

"What's his name?" Alexandre's deep murmur seemed to reach the child, for he stopped crying and hiccuping, blue eyes curious. "Hello, little one."

The mother was smiling in relief. "Oh, I should've

thought of that—his father's voice always calms him. Could you please just talk to him for a while?"

Instead of painfully waiting away the time it took for the nurse to find the files, Charlotte watched in delight as Alexandre revealed an aspect of himself that she never would've guessed. Not only was he willing to accommodate the mother's request, he spoke to the baby with tenderness that betrayed a genuine liking for children.

When her turn to see the doctor arrived, the woman thanked them both. "You should have a few of your own," she told Alexandre. "They'd be pretty as pictures what with her gorgeous skin and your eyes." Laughing at Charlotte's blush, she gathered up her things and left.

The feel of Alexandre's knuckles rubbing her cheek had Charlotte turning. He was smiling at her. "Would you like to have my *bébé, ma petite?*"

"I'd like to be married first." She teased him back despite her blush. "And we both know that's not a likely option between the two of us."

Until the stranger's laughing advice, Charlotte had never even allowed herself to imagine a lifetime with Alexandre. She'd fight for whatever he could give her, fight for more than this month, but she had no hope that he'd be hers forever. No one could keep a man who didn't want to commit, to entrust a woman with his heart. And she would never be happy with only half of him.

His eyes darkened. "Perhaps we should talk about—"

"Well, that didn't take as long as I expected," a cheerful voice announced.

Charlotte's head jerked up toward Nurse Johnson as the woman took a seat beside her.

"The filing system's very good down there."

She wanted to tell the nurse to hurry but instead threaded her fingers through Alexandre's and tried to stay calm.

"Let's see." Nurse Johnson opened the file. Her eyes widened almost immediately. "It says here that Mary Ashton was injured in a car accident which killed her husband, but that she made a full recovery. She was released from this hospital a week after her admittance."

Charlotte just heard the word "released." Her whole body threatened to shake. "Th—thank you."

"Do you have any contact details for her?" Alexandre asked.

"I'm sorry—we just have the address in Kendall. And I can tell you that she doesn't live there anymore." The nurse stood. "I hope you find her."

Shocked, Charlotte just sat there after Ann Johnson left. Alexandre wrapped an arm around her. "Come, *chérie*." Grateful for his strength, she leaned on him as he walked her out of the hospital and to the car.

He didn't urge her to speak and it was only when they were driving out of the hospital that she said, "I never let myself think beyond finding out whether she'd lived or died. I never allowed myself to wonder why she gave us up when she loved us. I *know* she loved us. I remember!"

"Charlotte." Alexandre pulled the car off to the side of what appeared to be the main street, and reached out to cup her cheek.

She let him comfort her. "It hurts to know that all this time, she was in the world. All the times I needed a mother, she existed, but she didn't help me."

"*Couldn't* help you, *ma petite*. If what I've heard about Spencer is true, then he's a man capable of doing something as terrible as stealing an unwilling woman's children away from her."

She wanted to believe him, couldn't bear to think that her mother had walked away willingly. "Maybe. I only wish I knew where she was now."

"Doesn't look like things have changed much in this town over the years."

Nonplussed by what appeared to be an unrelated comment, she focused on the street. Kendall was flat, like so much of Nebraska. Spring had given the land a touch of green and the occasional tree bloomed pink and white, but the town itself was without character, the buildings coated with decades of dust. "No."

"Perhaps someone would remember your parents?"

Understanding his line of thought, she said, "It's a long shot but what can it hurt? We could ask them." She pointed to a threesome of elderly men sitting at a table outside a coffee shop. "They look like they've been there forever."

"It's worth a try. If they can't help, we could perhaps consult the town office."

Getting out, they crossed the empty street and made their way to the shop. It touched her that Alexandre accepted the hand she slipped into his without a word. In fact, his hand tightened firmly over hers.

When they'd almost reached the men, one of them squinted a pair of washed-out blue eyes and said, "Well, ain't that a sight? Haven't see anyone as pretty as you since Mary Little Dove moved away."

Charlotte froze. Disbelieving, she whispered, "You knew my mother?" Surely it couldn't be this easy?

He chuckled. "Little Charlotte Ashton, I'll be damned!" Slapping his thigh, he put his cards down on the table. "Didn't think we'd see you again after Mary sold up and headed out of town."

Obviously, the man thought she'd been living with her mother. She decided not to correct him. "That was…"

He scratched his head. "That would've been right after your father's death, now wouldn't it?"

One of the other men nodded. "Sad business, cut down in the prime of his life. Always liked David. Good man."

The father she'd never had a chance to know was suddenly a vivid picture in her mind. "Mama didn't keep in touch with anyone in this town, did she?" It felt strange to say Mama and know that somewhere out there, she did have someone whom she could call that.

"That's the God's truth. Heartbroken, she was. Just packed up and left and that's the last we heard of her." He smiled in memory. "Sure was a pretty little thing. All in all, though, I reckon it was a good thing she went back to her people—she needed some looking after."

The three elderly men started reminiscing about other things, already lost in their own world. Alexandre pulled her away. "You should eat something before we leave." It wasn't a suggestion, but an order.

"Do I look that bad?"

He led her into the shop. "You look lovely but you're neglecting yourself. I can't allow that."

The second they walked in, the waitress headed over. "You can pick your table—the lunch rush just finished," she said. "What can I get you?"

Charlotte let Alexandre order for her, her mind still abuzz with everything they'd learned. When the food arrived, she ate to placate Alexandre, but she couldn't have said what it was that she'd consumed.

An hour later, they left the town. "Heartbroken," Charlotte said softly. "Just over her husband or over losing her children, too?"

"You said she loved you," Alexandre's deep voice wrapped around her, making her feel safe and protected.

"I can remember her scent as she cuddled me, I can remember warmth. Yes, she loved us." Sighing, she laid her head against the backrest. "I hate Spencer. I hate him for whatever he did."

Her hands clenched into fists. "I know he gave us a good life and an expensive education, but if he stole my mother from me, then the price was too high."

Alexandre didn't attempt to pacify her, his hands capable as he drove the car. Somehow, she knew he not only understood her anger, he also supported her.

"I want to go see Spencer as soon as possible."

"Of course." Alexandre accelerated down the flat road, the land so empty that you could see for miles in every direction. "I'll inform the charter pilot of our change in plans. We can be in San Francisco by this evening."

Charlotte nodded, trusting him to get things done. The man had a presence that screamed capability. "No wonder people went crazy living here," she muttered. "I like land and space and sky, but this—it's magnificent and frightening at the same time."

"There's nothing to hide under," Alexandre added. "This is a place of truth."

Having found her own truth after so long, Charlotte couldn't disagree.

Alexandre waited until they were in the air before broaching a subject that had been preying on him for hours. "Charlotte, I want to talk to you about something very important."

"What?" Her eyes were clear and unhaunted when she turned to face him, her hair haloed by the light coming in through the window beside her.

He paused for a second to assess her condition. Though what they'd discovered was shocking, it was clear that the truth was erasing the pain she'd lived with for a lifetime. He decided that she was fully capable of hearing what he had to say.

"*Ma petite,* did you read the things I wrote to you?"

She blushed. "You know I did."

The memory of her response to his confessions heated his blood. "Do you think me a man who shares those thoughts with everyone?"

"No, of course not." Her puzzlement at his line of questioning was obvious.

"Then please explain to me why you've never considered marriage between us." Despite his attempt at calm, anger sparked off his every word.

"I—I…y-you…" She slapped her hands down on the seat. "I'm too emotionally distraught to talk about this right now."

"Chicken," he taunted, confident of her strength.

Her eyes narrowed. "I didn't consider it because I know your track record. You date gorgeous, elegant and sophisticated creatures and none of those relationships last longer than a few months.

"Not one of them succeeded in convincing you that a woman can be true to her man. I can't compete with them so how could I be expected to win commitment from you?"

He was amazed at her. "You are the loveliest woman I've ever known," he said. "Not only your face but your inner resources. The beauty you create with your hands, your loyalty and courage, your determination—*mon Dieu,* Charlotte, you don't have to compete with any other woman. You're in a category of your own."

"And what category is that?" she asked, her voice softer than the wind.

"The category occupied by my future wife, the mother of my children and my lover for life." He wasn't going to dance around this. The possessive tyrant in him had had enough subtlety. It was time to claim what was his.

The minute he'd written the first word of that letter to

her, he'd known that he'd fallen. And fallen hard. Whatever he'd tried to convince himself, that letter had been an invitation to much more than simple pleasure—it had been the key to his heart.

Only for his *petite* Charlotte could he have ripped himself open like that. And only this woman's reaction could've made the decision to bare his soul the most wonderful experience of his life.

He had every faith that she'd stick by him for life—Charlotte wasn't a woman who gave up on anything. Their visit to Kendall had only strengthened his belief. She was no more like his *Maman* and Celeste than he was like his father. Alexandre would never cheat his wife and children out of the love that was their right. And there was only one woman he could imagine in the position of his wife. Now, he just had to get her to agree to be his. Life without her was not something he even wanted to contemplate.

"Alexandre—are you proposing?" Big eyes became even bigger.

He glanced at the inside of the plane. "Forgive me, *chérie,* I'd intended to do this far more romantically, but this is the moment.

"I want you to be mine, Charlotte Ashton. I want you to take my name, sleep in my bed, spread your warmth into my home and love me for the rest of my life.

"I want you to give me daughters with your heart and sons with your spirit. But most of all, I want you to let me love you until the day I die."

Trembling, she reached out and touched his lips with her fingers. He kissed them gently, his heartbeat frozen as he waited for her response.

"Are you sure you want to marry me with everything that's going on in my life?"

"Ah, Charlotte, don't you know by now that I want you

to be mine, no matter what?" He spoke against those fingers, before reaching up to clasp that hand in his. "I'm dying here, *ma petite.*"

"Even before I knew you, I loved you." Her heart blazed in her eyes. "I promise you that my loyalty will never change. You don't ever have to worry that I'll be fickle or unfaithful."

He adored her for understanding so much about the shadows that haunted him. "*Oui,* Charlotte. I know this."

Her smile was so bright, it shattered his heart. "I can't believe I'm going to marry you."

"You're not allowed to change your mind."

"Never."

Feeling emotion choke his throat, Alexandre raised the arm of her seat and pulled her across into his embrace. She came, wrapping her arms tight around him, her face buried against his neck.

"I want to go away somewhere private with you and just love you," she whispered.

"But you have to find out the truth from Spencer," he completed, dropping a kiss on the raw silk of her hair. "I understand. We have a lifetime to love." The primitive in him sighed in contentment.

She was his.

Fourteen

They reached San Francisco just after six-thirty. By the time they'd found a hotel and checked in, it was almost eight. Charlotte was beginning to feel exhaustion seep into her bones, but was determined to seek out Spencer.

"Will he be at his office?" Alexandre queried, as they sat side by side on the sofa in their suite.

She frowned. "He works late."

"Perhaps you should wait till tomorrow."

"I want to get this over and done with."

"I know." He enfolded her in his arms. "But right now, you're tired and shocked. Your uncle seems like the kind of man who'd take advantage of that—unless you've changed your mind and would like me to accompany you to his office?"

She could hear his desire to be there for her in his voice. "No, I have to face him by myself. I can't explain it, I just have to. But you're right about him taking advantage of any weakness."

"Good. I'll drive you to Ashton-Lattimer tomorrow morning and wait nearby while you speak with him."

"I want to catch him early," she said, "before his staff comes in—Walker once said that he's usually in his office by eight. It's going to be bad enough as it is. I don't want to create a spectacle."

"I understand. We'll aim to reach there by eight." His hand stroked over her hair. "You're very tired."

"But not sleepy," she murmured, raising her head.

Dark eyes gleamed. *"Non?"*

"Non." A smile bloomed in her heart at the way he looked at her, as if she were all he'd ever wanted. "I could do with a bath, though."

"Am I invited?" He spoke against her lips.

She kissed him. *"Oui,* of course…if you order room service." Her teasing got her thoroughly kissed.

And then, it got her thoroughly loved.

The next morning, Charlotte said goodbye to Alexandre at the ground floor of Ashton-Lattimer and headed to the elevator. He'd accepted her desire to face Spencer alone, but had refused to stay at the hotel. They'd compromised by having him wait at a nearby coffee shop, from where he could see her when she exited the building.

A short elevator ride later, she was standing in the outer part of Spencer's office. Stationed to the left of the door that led to his inner sanctum was a desk she assumed belonged to his secretary. It was an elegant curve against the wall, its surface pristine. However, on closer inspection, she saw that the back, hidden from the public, was buried in papers, cups, stationery and other miscellaneous items.

For some reason, it gave her courage that Spencer's

secretary wasn't a perfect robot. Squaring her shoulders, she took a deep breath and shoved open the closed door to his office. Surprise was her friend with the manipulative man who'd stolen her mother from her.

There was no one in the room.

Her heart plummeted. Wanting to throw something, she looked around for a chair where she could wait for him. That was when her eye fell on what looked like a jacket lying behind Spencer's executive chair. Except…there was something wrong with it, something that sent her nerves screaming with primitive terror.

Mouth dry, breath locked in her throat, she rounded the edge of the desk. All the air left her lungs in a harsh gasp, leaving her perilously close to fainting. But the thought of landing *there* snapped her back almost before the thought entered her head.

Spencer *was* in his office.

His body lay lifeless on the floor, appearing smaller and weaker than she remembered, his dominating personality extinguished. He'd fallen onto his back, his jacket parting to reveal a shirt stained dark with blood. More blood had congealed around him, turning the muted carpet almost black. Even to her untrained eye, it was chillingly clear how he'd met his end.

Spencer Ashton had been shot through the heart.

Shaking, she bent to touch his pulse, though she knew it was a futile effort.

"Mr. Ashton, I have…"

The feminine voice trailed off as Charlotte rose from behind the desk. She didn't have the energy to be startled, caught in a slow-moving river of emotion that was as thick as treacle. "He's dead."

Stunning violet eyes widened. "What?"

"Spencer is dead. Call the police."

The sharply dressed blonde walked over as if she didn't believe Charlotte, her legs long and slender beneath her severe navy suit. "Oh, my God." Her eyes fell on the body, then flashed up to Charlotte, suspicious.

"I'm Charlotte Ashton." She moved away from the body, taking the other woman with her. "Spencer is…was, my uncle."

"I'm Kerry, Mr. Ashton's administrative assistant."

"I just came to talk to him," Charlotte found herself saying. "Only a minute before you, I walked through that door and he was already dead."

"I guess it could just as well have been me." Kerry paused. "You really don't look much like a murderer anyway."

Charlotte didn't know why but both of them found that hilarious. Laughing, they hugged each other until they trembled. "I think we're hysterical," she said, when she was finally able to speak.

"Let's get out of this office." Kerry's voice quivered with more than a trace of shock. "We'll call the police from my desk."

Avoiding looking at the body, they walked out. Aware that they shouldn't disturb the scene any more than they already had, they left the door open.

Once they'd made the call, they sat together in silence. Charlotte fought the urge to contact Alexandre on his cell phone—the police had asked both her and Kerry to refrain from getting in touch with anyone else until they arrived. It didn't stop her wishing that he was by her side.

In under half an hour, the entire floor was swarming with police officers and crime-scene technicians. When they'd first entered, Charlotte and Kerry were asked their names and then told to wait by Kerry's secretly messy desk.

Ten minutes later, a striking man with dark hair stopped

in front of them. Accompanying him was a woman of average height, but with a suggestion of muscle about her. Neither was in uniform.

"I'm Detective Dan Ryland and this is my partner, Detective Nicole Holbrook." The man's eyes seemed to bore right through them. "Which one of you found the body?"

"Me," Charlotte said. "I came in to talk to him and he—he was just lying there." She'd never seen anything like that. The violence of it still had her shaking.

"If I could talk to you alone?" Detective Ryland's manner was efficient, but she knew he had to view her as a potential suspect.

She followed the two detectives after sharing a speaking look with Kerry, whose shock-bleached face told her what her own must look like. "Of course."

"Ms. Ashton, it's almost certain that the autopsy will confirm that Spencer Ashton died sometime last night. The blood..." Detective Ryland paused, his hazel eyes astute.

She could imagine hardened criminals confessing under the focus of that stare, but it barely penetrated her traumatized mind. "I've never seen anybody lose that much. I didn't know a person had that much in them."

Detective Holbrook touched her hand. "You've had a shock. Just hold on for a little while." Intelligent blue eyes watched her sympathetically from behind wire-frame spectacles.

Detective Ryland flipped open a notebook. "If I could eliminate you straight away, it would simplify matters. Where were you last night and early this morning?"

"I was in a hotel last night." She named the hotel. "I arrived here just before eight this morning. Security downstairs was trying to call up to tell Spencer I was coming, but I didn't wait for them."

"Were you alone in the hotel?"

Relief whispered through her. Because of one special man and the hope he'd brought into her life, she'd never be alone again. "I was with my fiancé. His name is Alexandre Dupree."

As his name left her lips, there was a commotion near the elevator. And suddenly, Alexandre was striding toward her, determination stamped on every line of his face. The cops trying to stop him didn't seem to know what to do against his strength of purpose.

All at once, she knew she'd been waiting for him, aware that nothing would keep him from her side once he realized that something had happened. Without hesitation, she flowed into his arms when he reached her.

"Are you all right?" His face was taut.

"I'm fine." And she was. A little shaky, still rocked by the violence she'd seen, but deep inside where it mattered, she was okay.

"What happened? I saw all these police officers when I decided to wait for you downstairs."

She smiled at his impatience, but before she could answer, Detective Ryland interrupted. "Where were you last night, Mr.…?"

"Dupree, Alexandre Dupree." Alexandre glanced at the open doorway to Spencer's office. "And I was with Charlotte last night. The hotel staff will verify that."

Something flared in Charlotte's brain. "We ordered room service and then there was that fax that got delivered to us by mistake after we'd gone to sleep."

"*Oui.* Several people can attest to our presence at the hotel for the entire night."

Detective Ryland closed his notebook and said, "You're free to go for now, but we may have further questions for you at a later date. In case you haven't guessed, Mr. Dupree, we're investigating a serious crime—the murder of Spencer Ashton. I'd appreciate your cooperation."

"You can reach us at the Ashton Estate, with the rest of the Ashton family," Alexandre answered.

The detective nodded. "Please don't contact anyone else about this—we'll take care of that."

Charlotte had been thinking about calling Walker. "When will you...?"

"Don't worry. It'll be very soon." With that, they moved onto Kerry, standing only a foot or so away.

"Who is that?" Alexandre asked, his tone low.

"Kerry, Spencer's admin. Let's wait and take her with us when we go—she might not want to be alone." She blinked as something Kerry was saying caught her attention.

"...they were arguing. It sounded ugly—I could hear them through the office walls."

Detective Ryland's whole posture changed. "That's Grant Ashton?"

"Yes." Kerry nodded, violet eyes looking bruised in her pale face. "According to my schedule, he was Spencer's last appointment for the day. But, he can't have done *that*." Her voice trembled at the end.

"Why?" Detective Holbrook asked, her tone softer than her more abrasive partner's.

Kerry looked at the woman. "Well, Spencer was still alive when Grant left."

Detective Ryland wrote that down but the look of intense interest on his face didn't fade. "Was Grant Ashton calm when he left?"

"N-no. He was pretty angry—furious..."

The noise of several technicians leaving Spencer's office drowned out the rest of the interview. Alexandre leaned down to whisper in Charlotte's ear. "Grant?"

"He's Spencer's eldest son from his first marriage." The implications of what Kerry had revealed made her heart race. "I don't know him but I can't imagine..."

Alexandre murmured soothingly and stroked her back. "The truth will come out. It always does."

Given what she'd discovered only hours ago, Charlotte agreed with him.

"Am I glad that's over." Kerry's relieved exclamation broke into her thoughts. "Thanks for waiting. I needed the support."

"You're welcome. We'd be happy to give you a ride home," Alexandre offered.

The other woman shook her head. "Thanks, but I think I'll take a walk."

"Are you sure?" Charlotte asked, worried.

Kerry nodded. "Some fresh air will do me good."

They parted on the ground floor, both of them deep in thought over what they'd witnessed.

By the time Charlotte and Alexandre arrived home, the estate was in an uproar, news of Spencer's death having beaten them to Napa. Lilah was a complete wreck.

Charlotte left Alexandre's side to help Megan and Paige calm the older woman. Lilah finally slept sometime in the small hours of the morning and instead of going to the cottage, Charlotte collapsed in Alexandre's room.

Nobody said anything about the arrangement and even if they had, it wouldn't have mattered. It wasn't a night to be alone, especially when the man she loved was more than willing to hold her through the dark hours.

The next morning, they drove a golf cart to her cottage so she could shower and change, before returning to the main house to join the others in the breakfast room.

Lilah appeared calm, but both Paige and Trace had dark circles under their eyes. Walker, who'd arrived late last night, seemed to be in shock. Megan looked marginally better—she'd spent the night in her own home and driven over with Simon early this morning. Charlotte had a feeling that Megan had only returned to the tense atmosphere of the house because it was obvious that Paige needed support.

After Lilah excused herself to go sit in the library, the rest of them stared at each other, not knowing what to say.

It was Walker who broke the silence. "I'm sorry you had to go through that, Charlotte."

"I wasn't alone," she said softly, glad that Walker and Alexandre were getting along. She'd introduced them last night and while Walker had been surprised by their engagement, he'd made no negative comments. It mattered to her that the two most important men in her life accept each other.

"What a mess," Trace muttered. "And it's only going to get worse. No one knows what he put in his will."

"Your father's not even buried and you're worried about the will?" Walker's tone could've cut glass.

Trace's eyes sparked with anger. "We have to worry. It's not only the vineyard that's at stake but Ashton-Lattimer, too. With Spencer dead, do you really think the others are going to sit back?"

At the mention of Spencer's two ex-families, silence descended on the table. The doorbell rang in the distance. A minute later, the housekeeper entered the breakfast room and leaned down to speak to Charlotte, who happened to be sitting nearest the door.

"Mercedes Ashton and Jillian Ashton-Bennedict are waiting in the front gallery." Irene kept her tone low.

"Thanks. Paige, Megan," Charlotte said, thankful for Irene's discretion. "We've got visitors."

When the men looked up, she attempted a smile. "Girls only." Kissing Alexandre on the cheek, she walked out with the others. "It's Mercedes and Jillian."

Megan brightened but Paige continued to look subdued.

When they reached the gallery just off the entrance, Jillian immediately headed over to meet them, graceful as always. "We heard what happened—we just came to say that if you need anything…"

"Thanks for coming," Megan said. "This is going to be a big mess, but at least the women are willing to talk."

Mercedes, always slightly reserved, nodded. "I'm worried—"

Before she could finish her sentence, a high voice screamed, "Get out!"

Whirling around, Charlotte found herself looking at Lilah. The redhead's usually cool, emotionless face was suffused with rage and she clutched a cut-glass tumbler as if she wanted to throw it. "Get the hell out of my house!"

"Mrs. Ashton," Jillian began, her tone gentle.

"He's not even buried and you've come to gloat?" Lilah cried. "Get out! Get out! Get the hell out!"

Paige went to her mother but Lilah shook off her hand. "Leave!" Striding to the entrance, she hauled open the door and pointed. "Get out."

Charlotte touched Jillian's arm. "I'm so sorry."

"It's okay," Jillian whispered. "I'll call you later."

The two women left without another word. Lilah slammed the door behind them and stalked back into the library, the tumbler still in her hand. It was only then that Charlotte realized the other woman had been drinking.

Late that night, she finally had a moment alone with the man she adored beyond reason. "Alexandre," she whispered, as they were getting into bed at the cottage, preferring the privacy it afforded over the estate house.

"*Ma petite?*" His masculine voice was a purr in the darkness.

"With everything that's happened the search for my

mother's been pushed into the background." She settled into the bed.

He slipped in beside her and cuddled her close. "But not forgotten. We know your mother left Kendall and returned to her people. It's not much but…"

"But if Spencer wasn't lying to me, my mother originally came from the Pine Ridge reservation."

"It makes sense to start your search there."

"Where else could she go—a woman who'd lost everything?" A lump lodged in her throat. "It can't be done from a distance. We'd have to go to Pine Ridge."

"Does it have to be you, Charlotte? Can you not hire an investigator?" Alexandre's voice was coaxing but not demanding. "You've endured much this past week—it hurts me to see you hurting," he admitted, shattering her completely. "I'd like to take you away from here for a while, show you my homeland, have you meet my *maman*."

The idea tugged at Charlotte's heart. "I'm tired of this place, too," she confided. "I want to meet your mother. But I don't want to give up on my own mother when I'm so close. I feel like I can almost touch her."

They were both silent for a while.

"If this is what you need to feel happy, then of course we'll stay in America and go to Pine Ridge," Alexandre began.

"I told Walker about our mother today." Charlotte couldn't forget the ravaged look that had dawned in her brother's eyes as she'd spoken.

"When?"

"After lunch, while you were talking with Trace. I had to tell him in private. And I wanted to do it before he spent too much of himself grieving for a man who didn't deserve his loyalty. You understand?"

"Of course. I realize what a shock it must've been. He, I believe, was very close to Spencer."

"Yes. He looked up to him, respected him, trusted him." She hated that Spencer was causing her beloved brother pain even from beyond the grave. "I was thinking…"

"Yes?" The single word was a stroke in the darkness.

"We can help with the research, but maybe Walker should be the one to go to Pine Ridge. He needs to do this, just like I needed to find out the truth."

"And how would that make you feel? You were the one who believed, but he'll probably see her first."

Charlotte smiled. Trust Alexandre to think of her welfare. "I want to meet her so desperately, but I love Walker. I can give him this because if the situations were reversed, I know he wouldn't hesitate."

Alexandre's hand spread on her stomach, warm and protective. "Then do you wish to remain here for Spencer's funeral?"

"I'm no hypocrite. I never liked him and if there were any choice, I wouldn't stay. But given the way Lilah's acting and the mess things are already in, I have to support the others at least through the funeral." She bit her lip. "Am I a terrible person for not being sorry he's dead?"

"No, you're simply honest. This man caused you only pain. Why should you mourn him?" He kissed her.

Her returning kiss held her heart. "Thank you."

"Then shall I book our tickets once we know the funeral arrangements? I'm sure we'll be given permission to leave after those detectives check out our alibi with the hotel staff."

"Yes." She frowned. "I just realized I'll have to find someone to take care of the greenhouse while we're in France."

He was quiet for a moment. "I want to ask you something about your greenhouse and this cottage."

"What?"

"If I had my way, I'd marry you right now. But, since we've decided to wait until things are calmer with the family, will you consider moving in with me when I establish a home in this country? It will be very soon—I want to get you away from the estate. From what I've seen, things are only going to get worse."

Smiling, she snuggled closer. "I'd love to move in with you but I can't abandon the greenhouse—it'd only put more stress on everyone."

"I understand, *chérie*. For the moment, we can find a house nearby so you can continue your work without being tied to the estate. Will that do?"

"It'll be perfect. And it won't be forever. I've always wanted my own business, independent of the Ashton name. Once things have settled down a little, I'll let the family know my decision to move on and we can decide where we want to live permanently."

"Maybe you can even do your work in France, *non?*" He turned to look down at her. This close, she could see his smile even in the darkness.

"Maybe." She smiled back. "Do you miss your home?"

"*Oui.* I worry about my vines."

"You're a winemaker to your toes." Her laugh bubbled out of her.

He chuckled. "You'll like my land in France. It's full of growing things." He dropped a kiss on the tip of her nose. "And I'm sure Paris will bespell you."

"Paris," she whispered. "I've always wanted to do something wild and romantic like run off to Paris."

"That wasn't in your journal. I would've noticed."

Joy whispered through her. No matter what happened in her life, so long as she had her wonderful Alexandre by her side, she'd flourish just like her flowers. "Don't you dare go near my journal again, Mr. Dupree."

"I won't need to."

"Why not?"

"Because, *ma petite,* I'm going to be such a wonderful lover, you won't be able to resist sharing your fantasies with me." It was a smug statement, but the tone was heart-breakingly tender.

Throwing her arms around him, she kissed him soundly on the lips. "I love you to bits, Alexandre Dupree."

"Then all my fantasies have come true."

* * * * *

Watch for the next book in
DYNASTIES: THE ASHTONS,
Estate Affair by Sara Orwig,
available in June from Silhouette Desire.

presents the next book in

Maureen Child's

miniseries

THREE WAY WAGER

*The Reilly triplets bet they could go
ninety days without sex. Hmm.*

WHATEVER
REILLY WANTS...

(Silhouette Desire #1658)
Available June 2005

All Connor Reilly had to do to win his no-sex-
for-ninety days bet was spend time with the
one woman who wouldn't tempt him. Yet
Emma Jacobsen had other plans, plans that
involved a *very* short skirt and a change
in attitude. Emma's transformation had
Connor forgetting about his wager—but
was what they had strong enough to last
more than ninety days?

Available at your favorite retail outlet.

Susan Crosby
presents the third book
in her exciting series

Where
unbridled
passions
are revealed!

SECRETS OF PATERNITY
(Silhouette Desire #1659)
Available June 2005

Caryn Brenley and P.I. James Paladin had a son
without ever meeing face-to-face *or* skin-to-skin.
When Caryn uncovered James as her child's sperm
donor, she reluctantly agreed to let father and
son meet. James jumped at the opportunity, but
pretty soon he wanted to get close to Caryn—
the natural way.

Available at your favorite retail outlet.

COMING NEXT MONTH

#1657 ESTATE AFFAIR—Sara Orwig
Dynasties: The Ashtons
Eli Ashton couldn't resist one night of passion with Lara Hunter, the maid at Ashton Estates. Horrified that she had fallen into bed with such a powerful man, Lara fled the scene, leaving Eli wanting more. Could he convince Lara that their estate affair was the stuff fairy tales were made of?

#1658 WHATEVER REILLY WANTS...—Maureen Child
Three-Way Wager
All Connor Reilly had to do to win his no-sex-for-ninety-days bet was spend time with the one woman who wouldn't tempt him. Yet Emma Jacobsen had other plans, plans that involved a *very* short skirt and a change in attitude. Emma's transformation had Connor forgetting about his wager—but was what they had strong enough to last longer than ninety days?

#1659 SECRETS OF PATERNITY—Susan Crosby
Behind Closed Doors
Caryn Brenley and P.I. James Paladin had a son without ever meeting face-to-face *or* skin-to-skin. When Caryn learned James was her child's sperm donor, she reluctantly agreed to let father and son meet. James jumped at the opportunity, but pretty soon he wanted to get close to Caryn—the natural way.

#1660 SCANDALOUS PASSION—Emilie Rose
Phoebe Drew feared intimate photos of her and her first love, Carter Jones, would jeopardize her grandfather's political career. So she went to Carter for help in finding them. But digging up the past also uncovered long-hidden passion, leaving Phoebe to wonder if falling for Carter again would prove to be her most scandalous decision.

#1661 THE SULTAN'S BED—Laura Wright
Sultan Zayad Al-Nayhal came to California to find his sister, but instead ended up spending time with her roommate, Mariah Kennedy. Mariah trusted no man—especially tall, dark and gorgeous ones. True, Zayad possessed all of these qualities, but he was ready to plead a personal case that even this savvy lawyer couldn't resist.

#1662 BLAME IT ON THE BLACKOUT—Heidi Betts
When a blackout brought their elevator to a screeching halt, personal assistant Lucy Grainger and her sinfully handsome boss, Peter Reynolds, gave in to unbridled passion. When the lights kicked back in, so did denial of their mutual attraction. Yet Peter found that his dreams of corporate success were suddenly being fogged by dreams of Lucy....